REED DESIGN
FOR
EARLY WOODWINDS

Publications of the Early Music Institute

Thomas Binkley, general editor

REED DESIGN
FOR
EARLY WOODWINDS

DAVID HOGAN SMITH

INDIANA UNIVERSITY PRESS

Bloomington and Indianapolis

The paper used in this publication meets the minimum requirements of
American National Standard for Information Sciences—Permanence of
Paper for Printed Library Materials, ANSI Z39.48-1984.

Manufactured in the United States of America

Library of Congress Cataloging-in-Publication Data

Smith, David Hogan.
  Reed design for early woodwinds / David Hogan Smith.
    p.   cm. — (Publications of the Early Music Institute)
  Includes bibliographical references and index.
  ISBN 0-253-20727-4
  I. Woodwind instruments—Reeds.   I. Title II. Series.
ML931.S64 1992
  788.5'19—dc20   91-38825

1 2 3 4 5 96 95 94 93 92

CONTENTS

To Susann

ACKNOWLEDGMENTS

Much of the material for this volume has been gathered over a number of years from many different sources. I am indebted to George Houle and Herbert Myers of Stanford University for their guidance during my studies there; and to Robert Cronin for his helpful advice regarding acoustic matters. I am also grateful to the members of The King's Trumpetts and Shalmes, whose diverse talents have provided a unique forum for learning and discussing some of the more practical aspects of wind playing. I am especially grateful to my wife, Susann, for her support and for patiently enduring the sounds of my reed-making experiments. The illustrations and music examples were done using CorelDRAW and Personal Composer software.

INTRODUCTION

As to the tone on . . . [the oboe and bassoon], much depends upon a good reed, that is, whether it is made of good and seasoned wood, whether it has the proper concavity, whether it is neither too wide nor too narrow, neither too long nor too short, and whether, when shaved, it is made neither too thick nor too thin. If the front of the reed is too wide and too long, the high notes become too low in relation to the low ones; but if it is too narrow and too short, they become too high. Even if all these conditions have been observed, however, the lips, and manner of taking the reed between the lips, are of even greater importance. You must not bite the lips in between the teeth too much or too little. In the first case, the tone becomes dull, in the second it becomes too blaring and strident.[1]

Thus Quantz neatly summed up in a single paragraph the main points of double-reed construction and embouchure formation for the eighteenth-century oboe and bassoon of his time. The details of reed making described here by Quantz are the same ones that all of us have struggled with at one time or another, whether it involved making a reed for a modern bassoon or making a reed for a Renaissance shawm. Unfortunately, very little direct information about reed making exists before the late eighteenth century, and we must therefore draw upon much indirect information in order to design and construct appropriate reeds for instruments of earlier times.

Double reeds are formed from the walls of the grass *Arundo donax*.[2] Native to the areas along the Nile River and to the countries surrounding the Mediterranean Sea, *Arundo donax* can now be found in all subtropical and warm-temperate areas of the world. Most of the cane used in modern reed making comes from southern France, where it is cultivated specifically for this purpose.

Arundo donax is a natural resource that has had a profound significance on the historical development of Western European woodwind instruments, from their roots in the Egyptian and Middle Eastern cultures to the present day. Its structure is unique among plant materials and provides an ideal substance from which to fashion the sound generators of woodwind instruments. This is due primarily to its resilience and responsiveness to changes in embouchure pressure as well as its ability to tolerate contact with moisture without adverse effects. Because of these attributes, a suitable alternative has yet to be found, although such exotic materials as boxwood, ebony, heather root, lancewood, teakwood, celluloid, hard rubber, synthetic resin, ivory, and silver have been tried during times of cane

Figure a. Making a double reed.

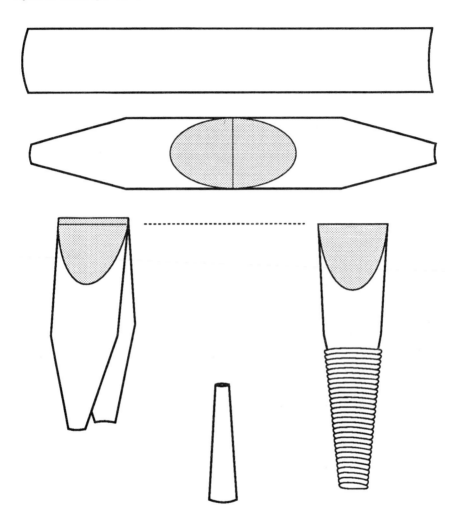

shortage.[3] Plastic has been used for crumhorn reeds, but most performers have concluded that they are not very satisfactory, at least from the viewpoint of tone quality.

The general construction of all types of double reeds is exemplified by the design of the reed for a bagpipe chanter as shown in Figure a.[4] Double reeds are fashioned from a section of cane tube which is first weakened in the center and

Figure 6. Designation of pitches.

then folded in half and bound with string at the base. Some reed styles (such as bagpipe reeds and oboe reeds) are bound to a metal staple which is then inserted into the instrument, while other styles are formed separately on a mandrel and are thus detachable from a conical metal staple. The cane is cut open at the tip, and the blades are further weakened by scraping until a desired result is obtained.

Because modern reeds are still constructed from the same plant material as reeds of earlier times and because the methods of construction have not changed significantly, the main intent of this reed-making manual has been to codify the various reed parameters available to both the reed maker and the performer in order to better understand and control double-reed behavior. This has been accomplished by first examining the acoustic requirements of double reeds in general and then applying this knowledge to reed designs for specific groups of early instruments.

Chapters 1 through 4 are intended primarily as the reference material upon which the remainder of the manual is based, and these chapters should be perused whenever more detailed information is needed concerning reed-making techniques, types of tools, or reed design. Chapters 5 through 8 deal more specifically with the different styles of reeds for Renaissance woodwinds and the particular problems associated with each style. Sample reed measurements have been provided in these chapters for the primary families of early woodwinds. Workable reeds for most nonstandard instruments and for bagpipe chanters can be designed and constructed from these measurements by applying the principles of reed design as outlined in Chapter 1. A brief list of mail-order sources for cane, tools, and double-reed supplies is found in the Appendix.

A simple system for designating fingerings has been employed and consists of the following: 123 4567 (counting from the top of the instrument). A dash (–) or the absence of a symbol indicates an open hole; a slash (/) through a number indicates that the hole should either be leaked or partially closed, depending upon the situation. If an instrument has a thumbhole, it has been indicated by the symbol "Th." The additional finger holes and keys found in certain families of instruments have not been indicated.

The pitch notation used throughout this manual follows the system used by the Acoustical Society of America and accepted by the U.S.A. Standards Association. It is based on the numbering of octaves as they occur on a standard piano keyboard, beginning with the lowest C. The pitch ranges are given in Figure b.

REED DESIGN
FOR
EARLY WOODWINDS

I

ACOUSTICS

Introduction

Even the most basic elements of musical acoustics can seem unnecessarily complicated to musicians, whose task is really not the scrutiny of the physics of sound but that of recreating an aural art. All double-reed woodwinds, whether they be Renaissance or modern ones, comprise a rather complex acoustic system of which the reed is only one component. This system becomes even more intricate through the interaction of the reed with the performer. When making double reeds, therefore, it becomes necessary to understand some of the basic acoustic principles of instrument design. All of us have experienced the time when the only reed for a particular instrument cracked or finally died of natural causes, and we were left with the task of making a new reed without a working one to copy. Since good reed design involves much more than merely duplicating the exterior dimensions of the reed, it is hoped that the principles outlined here will better enable prospective reed makers both to design appropriate reeds for their instruments and to adjust and optimize the reeds they are currently using.

The study of musical acoustics is a rather recent historical phenomenon, and because of its complexity even today many details await further investigation.[1] Historically (and even to the present day) musical instruments have been developed empirically. This has involved a long and gradual process of refinement of design through experimentation, educated guesses, and satisfying the musical needs of the performers for which they were built. Even with our present knowledge of acoustics, this approach often still proves to be the most useful and expedient. This is especially true in reed making. One can meticulously copy an old reed, duplicating all the external measurements, the type of scrape, and so forth, but actually playing a few notes on the new reed will reveal more about its acoustic characteristics than any other type of scientific evaluation.

Because of the nature of our sense of hearing, a musical tone is perceived to have a combination of a fundamental frequency plus greater or lesser amounts of

Figure 1.1. The harmonic series of C_3.

higher frequencies which are related integrally to this fundamental frequency. For example, a tone with a frequency of 100 Hz and containing partials at frequencies of 200, 300, 400, 500, etc., Hz will be perceived as a stable musical tone. This relationship of pitches is known as the harmonic series and is given in Figure 1.1 for the note C_3.

If a pure tone of 100 Hz is generated without any upper partials, our ears will sample the tone at the upper harmonic frequencies and create within our hearing perception partials at those frequencies, even though they do not physically exist. Similarly, if upper partials are generated without a fundamental, our sense of hearing will attempt to organize the components as though a fundamental did exist, and we will perceive the pitch as being that of the missing fundamental.

While the partials of a tone need not be integrally related (as is the case with many types of percussion instruments), those which closely match the relationship of the harmonic series are the ones which are considered desirable in woodwind tone production. The particular strength and distribution of the upper partials of a musical tone thus determine its timbre. If the upper partials of a tone are weak or are not exactly related to the fundamental pitch in an integral fashion, we generally perceive the tone as being dull or stuffy. On the other hand, a tone with strong upper partials that are related integrally is heard as being bright and resonant. It therefore becomes apparent that the best musical instruments, from both the listener's and the performer's points of view, are the ones whose pitches contain a reasonable amount of upper partials that are aligned with one another in a harmonic (i.e., integral) fashion.

Acoustically speaking, a double-reed woodwind consists of three interacting parts: the reed, the bore, and the tone holes. The reed serves as the tone generator for the system. As air from the lungs is forced through the reed, the increased flow of air draws the tip of the reed closed and releases a puff of air into the bore of the instrument. The strength of the natural arch of the blade in turn pulls the tip of the reed open, resulting in a valvelike action. As the continued flow of compressed air from the lungs again forces the reed closed, the cycle is repeated. The pitch we perceive in this modulated air stream depends on the rate at which the puffs of air are emitted.

The double reed is attached to the bore of the instrument, which acts as a resonator. When all the finger holes are closed, the pressure wave created by the reed travels down the bore to the bell section, where a small amount of the wave energy is "leaked" into the room and gives rise to a musical tone. Most of the wave, however, is reflected into the instrument. As the wave returns to the reed cavity, a point of maximum pressure is created in the reed. This forces the reed open and allows it to emit another puff of air into the instrument. The reflected waves thus combine with those produced by the reed to form a "standing wave" in the bore of the instrument. In this manner the bore determines the frequencies at which the reed can oscillate to sustain a tone.

The player can change the acoustic length of the instrument by uncovering the finger holes. This effectively shortens the standing wave pattern and thereby raises the pitch as holes are successively uncovered. Most double-reed woodwinds also have open-standing resonance holes in the bell section which are not fingered[2] but nevertheless provide some important acoustic functions by reinforcing the higher partials of standing-wave patterns, as we shall see later.

The Bore Design

Of all the bore shapes that might be imagined, two types prove to be musically useful for the double-reed woodwinds: the expanding cone and the cylinder.[3] These shapes are illustrated in Figure 1.2. In fact, a bore that is not strictly cylindrical or conical will still behave for musical purposes as though it were a modified version of one of these two designs.

Figure 1.2. Woodwind bore shapes.

(a) cylindrical   **(b) conical**

Among the Renaissance families of double-reed instruments having an expanding bore are the shawm, the curtal, and the *Rauschpfeife*. Those types with a cylindrical bore include the crumhorn, the *Rackett*, and the *Sordun*. In addition to having an expanding bore, the shawm and the curtal are blown with the lips placed directly on the reed, while the reed of the *Rauschpfeife* is covered with a cap. Of the cylindrically bored instruments, the crumhorn employs a capped reed, while the *Rackett* and the *Sordun* are direct-blown. These relationships are given in Table I.[4]

TABLE I. **Bore shapes and reed generators of early woodwinds.**

CYLINDRICAL BORE	CONICAL BORE
Capped reed:	Capped reed:
Crumhorn	*Rauschpfeife*
Uncapped reed:	Uncapped reed:
Rackett	Shawm
Sordun	Curtal

Because of the nature of the tone generator and its resonator (i.e., the reed and the bore), various modes of vibration can coexist within the instrument. These different modes of vibration are known as air-column resonances, or bore modes, and instruments having resonances which are integrally related under playing conditions are the ones that are musically useful.

In cylindrically bored instruments the air-column resonances occur at odd multiples of a fundamental; i.e., they are 1, 3, 5, 7 . . . times the fundamental frequency. This relationship proves musically useful, since these partials are among those our ears listen for in musical tones. Although the reed produces both even and odd harmonics, only the odd harmonics of its tonal recipe are amplified by the bore. The relative strength of the odd-numbered partials (compared to the weak, even-numbered ones) gives cylindrically bored instruments their characteristic "hollow" tone color.

On the other hand, the air-column resonances of an expanding bore have been compressed so that they occur 1, 2, 3, 4 . . . times the fundamental frequency. A conical bore thus amplifies all the harmonics generated by the reed. This strengthening of both odd and even harmonics in the tone of a conically bored instrument provides it with its own characteristic tone color.

An instrument that is the stablest in pitch (as well as being the easiest to play) is one in which the air-column resonances employed by the various notes are matched as closely as possible to integral relationships. Such perfect alignment, however, is seldom realized on an actual instrument throughout its entire scale, and the degree of misalignment of air-column resonances for a particular note will be discernible by its tone quality and/or stability. The particular combination and strength of air-column resonances that are excited when a tone is produced and stabilized has been termed a "regime of oscillation" by Benade.[5]

For various reasons the designs of many Renaissance woodwinds involve compromises in order to maintain harmonic alignment for good stability. One such method involves making small changes to the bore shape. A localized enlarging or narrowing of the bore, for example, will alternately raise or lower the upper partials in the region of the notes it affects. A more broadly distributed change in the bore, on the other hand, will have a greater effect upon the fundamental pitch of a note than upon its upper partials. Enlargements and constrictions at various points in the bore are used to compensate for finger holes which cannot be placed in their ideal acoustic location, especially on larger instruments.

The Tone Holes

Before detailing the properties for good reed design, we will first examine some of the acoustic properties of woodwind tone holes.[6] Since the bore of a typical Renaissance woodwind (with its finger holes closed) can be made to produce only the lowest two or three of its harmonics, finger holes are arranged along the bore of the instrument to allow a musical scale to be filled in between these harmonics. The successive opening of holes along the bore effectively shortens the length of usable bore for tone production, and the instrument can thus be made to sound a progressively rising scale.

As sound waves travel down the bore of an instrument, most of the acoustic energy of the lower harmonics of the note is reflected into the instrument from the region just below the highest open hole, forming a standing wave at the frequency of each harmonic. These reflected waves help to stabilize the oscillations of the reed and give the note its characteristic timbre. There is a point above which the harmonics are no longer reflected but radiate freely from the open holes and the bell and consequently do not contribute much energy to the standing-wave pattern in the instrument. This frequency is known as the cutoff frequency. The cutoff frequency is determined by the nature of the tone-hole lattice and involves the size, number, and spacing of the tone holes.[7] An instrument with a constant cutoff frequency throughout its fundamental register is perceived as having a consistent timbre throughout its usable range and is therefore desirable.[8]

Since an instrument with a low cutoff frequency provides fewer air-column resonances for tonal stability, it is perceived by the player to be stuffy, less stable, or dull sounding. On the other hand, a similar instrument having a higher cutoff frequency allows the bore more control as a resonator, and this type of instrument is generally perceived by the player as being responsive, stable, brighter in timbre, and less sensitive to changes in the acoustic parameters of the reed.

The evolution of woodwind instrument design has been such that a modern woodwind generally has a cutoff frequency that remains fairly uniform throughout the first two octaves of its range. This frequency has been approximated by Benade for the modern, conically bored woodwinds as being the lowest frequency of the note fingered 123 −−−− on the instrument times a constant of 3.6.[9] Thus, the right-hand notes of the fundamental register have more upper resonances below the cutoff frequency to aid in providing stable regimes of oscillation than do the notes of the left hand.[10] The cutoff frequency for most of the early woodwinds with a conical bore is somewhat lower than this and usually lies in the region of two octaves above the fundamental note fingered 123 456−.[11] Renaissance woodwinds often have a less consistent cutoff frequency than do their modern counterparts, because of the compromise designs necessary for instruments which do not have full key mechanisms.

The exact size and placement of the tone holes also have some important implications.[12] In general, enlarging a tone hole or reducing its depth (through the use of narrower side walls) will raise its fundamental frequency and cause its upper partials to become more spread in relationship to the fundamental. Hence, the timbre generally becomes brighter, the pitch may become more stable, and a louder sound is produced. Conversely, reducing the size of a tone hole or lengthening its depth (through the use of thicker side walls) will lower its fundamental frequency, compress its upper partials, and produce a softer, duller, and less stable sound.

In larger instruments, finger holes are often bored at an angle through comparatively thick side walls in order to allow them to enter the bore of the instrument at a higher or lower position. This produces a tone hole with elongated side walls, as shown in Figure 1.3a. The undercutting of tone holes (enlarging the end of the tone hole as it enters the bore) is similar to enlarging the diameter of the hole and thus can allow a tone hole to be physically smaller at its external opening on the instrument than if an acoustically equivalent, cylindrical tone hole were used (see Figure 1.3b). Also, open keywork above a tone hole may flatten the pitch, depending upon its distance from the hole.[13]

All of these possible and often-used adjustments can have an effect on the cutoff frequency of an instrument and therefore on its general characteristic timbre. Enlarging an instrument's tone hole size in relationship to its bore size will raise the cutoff frequency and give the instrument a brighter timbre, while increasing

Figure 1.3. Woodwind tone-hole designs.

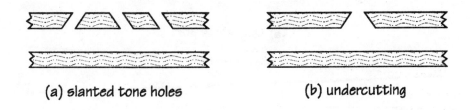

(a) slanted tone holes   **(b) undercutting**

the thickness of the walls of the instrument (i.e., deeper tone holes) or lengthening the space between tone holes will lower the cutoff, resulting in a duller timbre.[14] Thus, finger holes that need to be positioned away from their ideal acoustic positions for practical reasons can still be made to operate by altering their optimum size in a variety of ways, but sometimes at the expense of maximum stability or evenness of timbre, at least from the standpoint of our modern ears and expectations.

The Acoustic Functions of the Reed

Thus far we have examined some of the basic acoustic functions of the woodwind bore and its tone-hole lattice. The third, and perhaps most critical, component of a double-reed instrument is its tone generator, the reed. Acoustically speaking, the reed serves several purposes. As previously noted, it functions as a self-sustained oscillator to generate the acoustic energy necessary to activate the various resonances of the bore during tone production. In conically bored instruments, the reed also acts as the functional equivalent to the missing part of the cone on the upper end of the bore (see Figure 1.4) to provide proper alignment of the first and second air-column resonances for tone production in the fundamental octave. More importantly, the reed resonance (under playing conditions) aids in stabilizing the second register, strengthens upper partials that lie in its vicinity, and excites corresponding resonances of the standing-wave pattern in the bell section.

On a well-designed instrument the reed resonance and the equivalent volume of the reed have been adjusted so that both are properly placed and easily manipulated without requiring large embouchure changes. The less well they are coupled, the more difficult it becomes to change registers easily. A reed maker's time, then, is generally devoted to matching the equivalent volume of the reed to a particular instrument with subsequent fine adjustments in order to optimize

Figure 1.4. Acoustic and actual lengths of a conical woodwind. X_r and
X_{rs} are defined in the text.

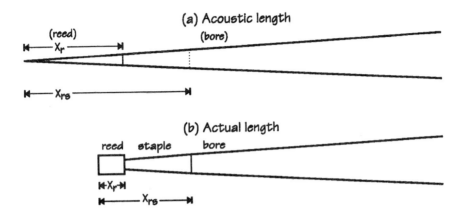

the flexibility of the reed resonance, whether it be an intuitive process or a con-
scious one.

The reed resonance may be described as the natural frequency of the reed
blades themselves. This is the pitch at which the blades would vibrate if they were
plucked like a tuning fork.[15] On shawm reeds, the reed resonance can be approximated by blowing on the reed alone. Although the volume of the air column inside the reed and its tube may have a slight flattening effect on the pitch of the
reed resonance, this test will still determine the vicinity of the actual frequency
being produced. Larger reeds and reeds having a long tube may sound somewhat
flatter than the actual pitch of the reed resonance.

For good cooperation with a conically bored instrument, the reed resonance
under playing conditions should lie in the region of two octaves above the low-
register note fingered 123 ––––, depending on the size and design of the instrument.[16] Thus, for a treble shawm in D, the pitch obtained by blowing the reed
alone to its highest possible pitch should be in the vicinity of A_6, or 1760 Hz. The
exact placement of the reed resonance for shawms and other instruments will be
discussed below.

Because the flexible walls and the tip opening of a double reed have a large
effect on its acoustic size, the physical size and volume of a reed are much smaller
than the actual length and volume of the part of the cone that it replaces. In conically bored instruments we can therefore speak of the equivalent volume of the
reed and the equivalent volume of the reed plus its staple as being those com-

binations which would closely approximate the corresponding missing parts of the cone under playing conditions. These are illustrated by the lengths X_r and X_{rs} respectively in Figure 1.4a.

In the case of the conically bored early woodwinds, the equivalent volume of the reed cavity remains fairly constant throughout the lower register of the instrument. This volume requirement is particularly important for the alignment of the first two resonances of a note when playing in the fundamental register. If the equivalent volume of the reed is too small, the fundamental will tend to be sharp in relation to the second partial, and all partials may drift sharp, causing a possible rise in pitch and less stability. Conversely, if the equivalent volume is too large, the fundamental will tend to be flat in relation to the second partial, and all partials may be noticeably flattened. These discrepancies are most apparent in the lowest notes of the instrument, where the missing part of the cone is small in relationship to the length of bore being used to sound the note.[17]

The lowest frequency of the reed-plus-staple combination, when the instrument is being played, should be the same as that of the lowest resonance of the missing part of the cone it replaces.[18] Thus, checking the joint playing frequency of the reed-plus-staple combination for a particular instrument provides a useful method for determining the proper equivalent volume of the reed. The reed-plus-staple joint playing frequency can be described by the rather simple formula $F_{rs} = V/2X_{rs}$, where V = the wave velocity of sound (about 347 meters per second for warm air) and X_{rs} = the length of the missing part of the cone.[19]

Another method for measuring the reed-plus-staple joint playing frequency (and one that is perhaps more accessible for musicians) is to determine the pitch produced by the reed and staple for a particular instrument, taking care to use the same embouchure as when the instrument is played. Since it is easy to lip this pitch around when only the reed and staple are involved, one should test it several times and, if possible, try more than one reed in order to ascertain the correct frequency.

In most woodwind designs, the joint playing frequency of a particular reed-plus-staple combination will lie at or very near the octave of the note fingered 123 −−−− on the instrument.[20] For example, the octave of the note fingered 123 −−−− on a treble shawm in D is A_5, or 880 Hz. Some experimentation by blowing the reed with its staple confirms that the particular shawm under consideration is best driven slightly above this frequency, at about $B\flat_5$ (932 Hz), for much of its range. Additionally, intentionally raising or lowering this frequency through excessive tightening or loosening of the embouchure causes the instrument to become less stable and less resonant in the lower octave because the reed-plus-staple driving system is no longer replacing the missing part of the cone with the parameters required for the best cooperation with the bore. The resonances in the regimes of oscillation being produced are less well aligned, and consequently the pitch goes correspondingly sharp or flat.

Knowing the reed-plus-staple driving frequency for a particular instrument can also be useful in determining correct embouchure formation for beginning players. By learning to sound the appropriate pitch with the reed and staple removed from the instrument, intonation problems or unstable notes that are caused by an incorrect embouchure can be often be eliminated.

While the interaction between the equivalent volume of the reed and the reed resonance is interlaced in a complicated manner, some generalizations about their effects can be made. As was noted, an appropriate equivalent volume of the reed is necessary primarily for correct intonation and attack of the scale in the lower octave and for proper alignment of the first and second bore modes of the fundamental scale.[21] A constant equivalent volume as detected in the reed-plus-staple joint playing frequency is dictated by the bore and is necessary for good cooperation and stability in the fundamental register of an instrument. The reed resonance can also serve to increase the stability of lower-octave regimes of oscillation. The partials of a low-register note that lie in the vicinity of the reed resonance (under playing conditions) will be greatly enhanced, and the regime of oscillation for that note will be additionally stabilized.

In the second octave, the placement of the reed resonance becomes critical for stabilizing the register. The reed resonance can be adjusted by minute changes in the embouchure over a range of as much as a fifth.[22] Additionally, the changes made to the reed resonance by an embouchure adjustment will have a much greater effect on the pitch of a second-register note than on the pitch of a note in the first register. For example, when the second-register note A_5 is sounded on the treble shawm in D, the experienced player automatically adjusts the reed resonance to A_6, an octave above the sounding pitch, as shown in Figure 1.5a. This enhances the regime of oscillation for A_5 and thereby adds stability and resonance to the note. Through extremely minute changes in the embouchure and/or breath pressure, manipulation of the reed resonance makes it possible to move the pitch of this note up or down very easily and much farther than doing the same manipulation of A_4 in the lower register.

From Figure 1.5a we see that the reed resonance for the treble shawm remains near E_6 for the entire first octave of the range of the instrument. The notes of this register are stabilized primarily through the proper alignment between the first two air-column resonances and depend upon the appropriate equivalent volume of the reed-plus-staple setup. In the second register, the gradual increase in the

Figure 1.5. Approximate resonances in shawms.

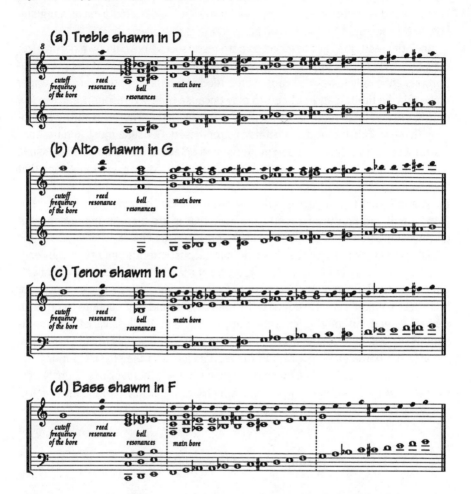

(a) Treble shawm in D

(b) Alto shawm in G

(c) Tenor shawm in C

(d) Bass shawm in F

frequency of the reed resonance (beginning with the note E_5) provides the primary stability for these notes through their octave alignment.

The higher reed resonance in this region of the scale also allows the upper-register notes to speak when using the same fingering as for the first octave. The slight change in embouchure and/or breath pressure needed to change octaves during playing serves to raise the reed resonance while at the same time weakening lower-mode cooperation. This cannot be easily done with the first overblown note (E_5), since the reed resonance is already aligned with the low-register note E_4. For this note, the first finger hole of the left hand is employed as a register hole and is opened tó produce the jump to E_5.

Since the reed does not respond to bore resonances above its own natural frequency,[23] it effectively limits the upper range of the instrument. If the reed proportions are overly large (i.e., causing the reed resonance to be lower), the upper range may be limited and difficult to play because the reed resonance is too low to help create stable regimes of oscillation in this range. Thus, the ability to produce these stabilizing upper partials is suppressed. Because most Renaissance instruments normally do not use more than an octave and a half of their possible range, instruments are often seen coupled with ill-sized reeds, usually ones that are too large. The result is a stuffy and unresponsive instrument with a limited range and sometimes an artificially lowered pitch. On the other hand, if the reed is too small and produces a reed resonance that is too high during low-register playing, some notes may tend to be sharp or to squeak easily.

Thus we have looked at the three primary acoustic requirements of the reed: (1) a suitably designed oscillator for tone generation, (2) a correct equivalent volume, and (3) an appropriate and flexible reed resonance. We can now investigate how these elements can be adjusted by reed design and embouchure to produce a suitable reed. Although there might appear to be an endless variety of combinations of reed, instrument, and embouchure that would satisfy these conditions, the acoustic parameters involved in the reed design and the physical limitations of *Arundo donax* actually place many restrictions on the general bore design. Nevertheless, numerous subtle adjustments which are musically significant are still possible.

Factors Involved in Reed Design

In order to understand more clearly which parts of a reed can be adjusted for optimum use with a particular instrument, we will first examine how a reed and staple must be proportioned to the bore in order to provide a musically useful system. For the best cooperation with the bore, the range of the reed resonance should be suitably located to provide optimal stability for a particular bore design. These ranges are given in Figure 1.5 for the shawm family. (The placement of the reed resonance in cylindrically bored instruments will be discussed below.) For the smaller sizes, the reed resonance is placed two octaves above the note fingered 123 456–, and it should additionally be flexible over a range of about a fifth above this.[24] For the bass shawm and the curtal, the reed resonance is placed approximately two octaves above the note fingered 12– –––––, because of its different bore design (see Figure 1.5d). The highest possible frequency of the reed resonance under playing conditions is determined primarily by the length and the taper (or lay) of the reed blades (length l in Figure 1.6). Although this length can vary among the reeds of individual players, the nature of *Arundo donax* is such that its relative longitudinal stiffness (which primarily determines the operating resonance frequency of the reed) is reasonably consistent for a given cane thickness, and therefore large deviations from a normal blade length for a given size of instrument are not possible.

By blowing a reed to its highest pitch with its blades undamped, we can approximate the highest possible reed resonance of the blades. In order for the reed resonance to be musically useful, however, it is actually somewhat lower than this and carefully controlled both by lip damping and by the size of the tip opening (distance o in Figure 1.6). These two factors determine the useful lower limit of the reed resonance under playing conditions on a finished reed. A reed tip which operates in a more closed state under playing conditions will raise the reed resonance and make it less flexible, while a more open tip will lower the reed resonance but allow more flexibility. These tip openings are shown in Figure 1.7.

The limits of the size of the tip opening are also determined by the amount necessary for good cooperation in the low register and the overall volume of sound desired. Closing down the tip of the reed (without altering other parameters) will cause the instrument to play more softly, and low notes may respond less well because of the raised reed resonance and the decreased equivalent vol-

Figure 1.6. The parts of a double reed.

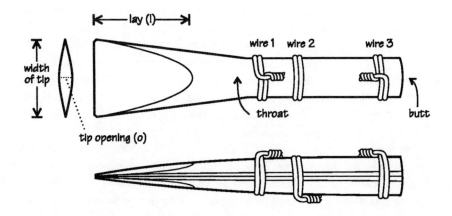

Figure 1.7. Tip openings for adjusting the reed resonance.

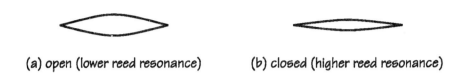

(a) open (lower reed resonance)   **(b) closed (higher reed resonance)**

ume. A more open tip, on the other hand, will generate a louder volume and favor the lower register because its lowered reed resonance is less well matched for upper-register playing unless a large embouchure adjustment is made.

The tip opening is controlled directly by the tightness of the embouchure and by the velocity of the air stream being blown into the instrument. Thus, using a loose embouchure will lower the reed resonance, as will blowing more gently (Figure 1.7a), while using a tighter embouchure or blowing harder will raise the reed resonance (Figure 1.7b). Players with strong embouchures generally prefer a wider tip opening, which is then closed down somewhat by the embouchure during playing. If the tip remains more open under playing conditions, the reed will generate more sound and require a stronger attack. Such a setup is less stable in pitch unless played at loud volume, but it does allow the player more control over dynamics through greater or lesser embouchure pressure to control the amount of tip opening. A larger tip opening will also increase the effectiveness of cross-fingered notes because both the reed resonance (for the upper register) and the equivalent volume (for the lower register) are more easily manipulated by subtle adjustments in the embouchure. Thus, a reed with an open tip is more tiring to play and difficult to control when it is played softly, but it allows the maximum possibilities of dynamic expression. Since the opposite holds for a more closed reed tip, a balance must be found for a particular embouchure which will provide maximum pitch stability, ease of blowing, and control over dynamics.

Lip damping involves the placement of the embouchure on the blades of the reed. (Damping should not be confused with embouchure tightness, or "biting." These embouchure parameters are discussed in more detail in Chapter 2.) If other parameters are left unchanged, placing the pads of the lips toward the top wire (i.e., placing more reed into the mouth) will raise the reed resonance and allow it to be varied over a larger interval. Conversely, playing with the lips toward the tip of the reed (i.e., placing less reed into the mouth) will lower the reed resonance and limit the interval over which it may be varied. These two extremes of embouchure formation are shown in Figure 1.8.

Additional considerations are taken into account by the shape of the reed. Nar-

Figure 1.8. Lip damping.

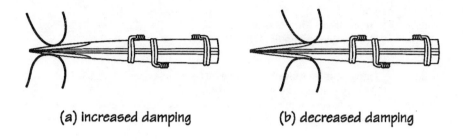

(a) increased damping   **(b) decreased damping**

Figure 1.9. Reed shapes.

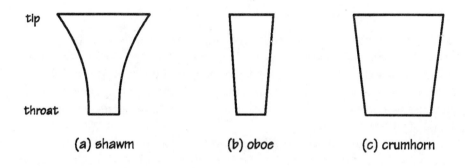

(a) shawm   **(b) oboe**   **(c) crumhorn**

rowness at the throat of the reed (Figures 1.9a and 1.9b) increases the flexibility of the reed blades available via embouchure manipulation and therefore allows greater control over the upper register through manipulation of the reed resonance. A wide throat (Figure 1.9c), on the other hand, favors stability of both the equivalent volume and the reed resonance and thus makes the lower register very stable and more difficult to overblow. A wide tip (Figures 1.9a and 1.9c) can provide more acoustic energy to the system and therefore a louder sound. This will also increase the stability of lower-register notes. Conversely, a narrow tip (Figure 1.9b) produces a quieter sound with fewer stabilizing effects in the low register. A reed with a tip that is wide in proportion to the length of its lay (such as fan-shaped shawm reeds) allows the reed resonance to be more flexible by its increased sensitivity to lip damping. This style of reed must be used in conjunction with a pirouette in order to provide stability. The general effects of the shape of the reed on response have been summarized in Table II.

When the desired length of lay, tip opening, and shape have been chosen ac-

TABLE II. **Factors for determining the shape of a reed.**

TIP
wide	more stable low notes; louder.
narrow	less stable low notes; softer.

THROAT
wide	more stable equivalent volume and reed resonance; fundamental register is very stable; does not overblow easily.
narrow	more flexible equivalent volume and reed resonance; both registers are less stable; upper register is less tiring.

SIDES
straight	more stable equivalent volume and reed resonance.
fanned	more flexible equivalent volume and reed resonance; louder.

cording to the above guidelines, the reed and its tube can then be coupled to a staple of appropriate length so that the combined equivalent volume of the reed and staple matches the volume of the missing part of the cone. This means that the lowest frequency of the reed-plus-staple driving system must match that of the missing part of the cone for maximum cooperation in the regimes of oscillation of the lower register.

The reed is therefore acoustically coupled to the proportions of the bore and the embouchure at three points. The first and second anchor points determine a careful placement of the upper and lower limits of the reed resonance under playing conditions, and the third anchor point allows for the proper tuning of the fundamental register. These main points have been summarized in Table III. Thus, the length of the reed blades (in relationship to the cane thickness) to a large degree dictates the position and tuning of the upper resonances of the instrument under playing conditions, while the width and flexibility of the reed blades are proportioned so that the notes of the lower register can be aligned to the more fixed positions of their upper partials.

Examples of the approximate proportions of reed size to bore length for shawms are given in Figure 1.10. The appropriate lengths for each section have been derived from the formula $F = V/2X$ (as previously described). Because the bores of actual instruments deviate from exact conicity, small deviations from the proportions given here are normal. It is noticeable from this illustration that the physical length of the reed and staple is much shorter than its acoustic length. The extreme flexibility of the reed cavity may also require slightly different proportions for different players in order to arrive at an equivalent acoustic result.

Figure 1.10. Approximate acoustic proportions for shawms.

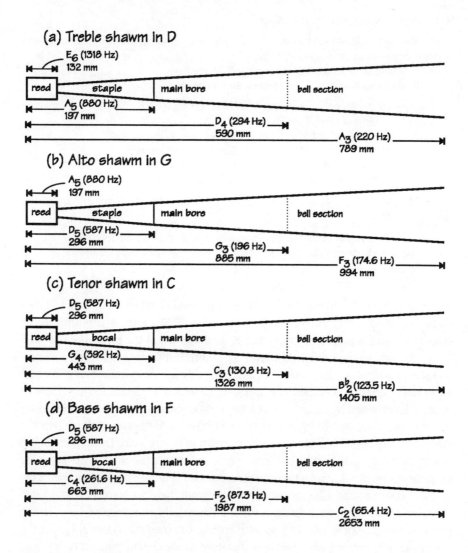

(a) Treble shawm in D

E₆ (1318 Hz)
132 mm

| reed | staple | main bore | bell section |

A₅ (880 Hz)
197 mm

D₄ (294 Hz)
590 mm

A₃ (220 Hz)
789 mm

(b) Alto shawm in G

A₅ (880 Hz)
197 mm

| reed | staple | main bore | bell section |

D₅ (587 Hz)
296 mm

G₃ (196 Hz)
885 mm

F₃ (174.6 Hz)
994 mm

(c) Tenor shawm in C

D₅ (587 Hz)
296 mm

| reed | bocal | main bore | bell section |

G₄ (392 Hz)
443 mm

C₃ (130.8 Hz)
1326 mm

B♭₂ (123.5 Hz)
1405 mm

(d) Bass shawm in F

D₅ (587 Hz)
296 mm

| reed | bocal | main bore | bell section |

C₄ (261.6 Hz)
663 mm

F₂ (87.3 Hz)
1987 mm

C₂ (65.4 Hz)
2653 mm

Because reed making for Renaissance instruments does not usually entail making staples and bocals as well, we do not need to concern ourselves with these details. It is worth mentioning, however, that the inner shape of the staple does have some acoustic effects. If a reed cavity is attached to a more conical staple (i.e., one having a greater rate of expansion), the upper resonances of the bore

TABLE III. **Acoustic points for designing a double reed.**

(1) Establish the range of the reed resonance.

> *Anchor point* 1: Determine the upper limit by a combination of the gouge thickness and the longitudinal stiffness of the blades:
> Thinner and/or longer lay = lower reed resonance
> Thicker and/or shorter lay = higher reed resonance

> *Anchor point* 2: Determine the lower limit by a combination of the size of tip opening and the amount of reed damping:
> Open tip = lower and more flexible reed resonance; louder
> Closed tip = higher and less flexible reed resonance; softer
> More damping = lower and less flexible reed resonance
> Less damping = higher and more flexible reed resonance

(2) Establish an appropriate equivalent volume for the reed-plus-staple setup to match the missing part of the cone.

> *Anchor point* 3: Add a proper length of reed tube and staple to the reed cavity to complement the bore for proper tuning of the notes in the fundamental register.

will tend to be more spread, while if the same reed is attached to a more cylindrical one, they will tend to be more compressed.[25] Since there is a limit to the amount of taper a staple can have, because of the size at the top of the bore and at the opening to the reed, this alteration is fairly subtle for smaller woodwinds.

A staple of unusual proportions or length could require an abnormally short (or long) blade length to compensate and thus be less than desirable. If a staple or bocal is lengthened by pulling it out a bit, erratic and undesirable situations may occur because of the enlargement created in the socket between the end of the staple and the beginning of the bore, as shown in Figure 1.11a. This type of setup is a modern one, although it is commonly found on copies of early instruments. Original instruments used a tapered staple socket (Figure 1.11b) rather than a cylindrical one, so that adjustments could be made here without leaving a large cavity to produce unpredictable results. Additionally, this type of lengthening (without making corresponding adjustments to the reed cavity) would lower the bore modes by varying amounts and therefore cause the instrument to feel less resonant.

When the reed-plus-staple setup is designed, it is imperative first of all to choose an appropriately sized blade length for a proper reed resonance, after which the staple is proportioned to the resultant equivalent volume of the reed cavity in order to supply the equivalent of the missing part of the cone. For example, Figure 1.12 shows two possible reed and staple designs for a treble shawm.

Figure 1.11. Fitting the staple into its socket.

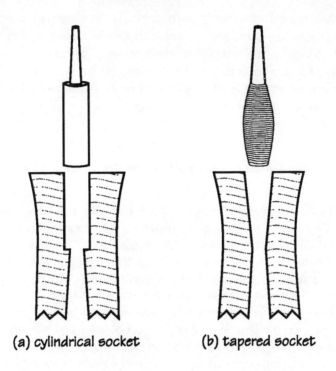

(a) cylindrical socket   **(b) tapered socket**

Figure 1.12. Cane-to-staple proportions.

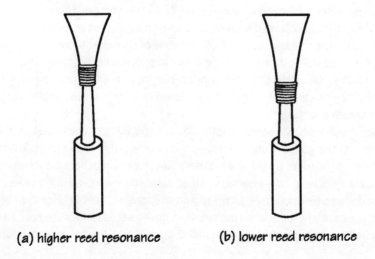

(a) higher reed resonance   **(b) lower reed resonance**

The first (Figure 1.12a) has a reed with short blades and a long staple, while the second (Figure 1.12b) has a reed with longer blades and a shorter staple. For both systems the reed-plus-staple driving frequency is the same ($B\flat_5$), but the range of the reed resonance of the second reed is about a fifth lower (A_5 to D_6) than the first reed. Placed on the instrument, the first setup operates normally as expected. The second plays in tune in the lower register but is duller in tone quality. In the upper register, however, the pitch is noticeably flat and unstable, almost to the point of being unplayable.

The Effects of Cane Stiffness on Reed Parameters

Since the longitudinal flexibility of the reed blades has a direct influence on the reed resonance, it follows that a small reed with very thin blades would be acoustically similar to a larger reed with thicker blades. This allows for a variety of shapes, all within certain limits, which will fit the proportions of a particular instrument. Musical requirements generally will dictate these boundaries. If the reed is quite thin, the instrument will be easy to blow in the low register, but the upper register notes become more difficult to overblow because the reed resonance has become too flexible to offer good cooperation and stability. This does allow for improved quality and efficiency in cross-fingered notes of the low register because the equivalent volume is also very flexible. In addition, the instrument will feel less stable because the embouchure can influence and alter the reed parameters very easily, leading to pitch fluctuations. This situation can be somewhat offset by the simultaneous use of a larger tip opening.

On the other hand, a reed with stiffer blades may be less responsive in the low register but may be easier to overblow because of its more stable reed resonance. Cross-fingered notes thus tend to be less effective and less stable. The stiffness of the blades also adds stability of pitch because they are not so easily dominated by the embouchure. The reed may, however, be more tiring to play or require higher breath pressure.

When considering these parameters, an additional option can be found in the thickness of the gouge. Cane closest to the bark is stiffer than cane taken nearer the center of the tube. By using a thinner gouge, one can benefit from some of the stabilizing effects of this relatively stiffer cane while keeping the blades rather thin and therefore more free-blowing and responsive. This is because the cane nearer the bark will retain the transverse stiffness necessary for the reed's role as an oscillator, even when the lay is scraped quite thin. Cane taken from nearer the center of the tube will lose much of its transverse springiness as it is scraped down and quickly become flabby and less resilient if it is scraped too thin. Since the quality of cane may vary from batch to batch, all of these parameters should be kept in mind when making a reed adjustment.

Adjusting the Acoustic Parameters of the Reed

Although the proper placement of the reed resonance is of primary importance when making a reed, it is not always easily determined or correctly assessed. If an instrument has been well designed, its bore and staple will usually dictate a reed of proper proportions so that both the reed resonance and the equivalent volume of the reed can be set to suitable values by the same embouchure. It is thus advantageous first to match the equivalent volume of the reed to the instrument and then to make any necessary adjustments as needed to improve the control of the reed resonance under playing conditions.

The equivalent volume of the reed is influenced by several factors. The obvious one is its total internal volume, as dictated by its physical size. In addition, the tip opening, the motion of the reed, and the stiffness and elasticity of the cane can all have an appreciable effect on the total equivalent volume.[26] In addition, the performance factors which can alter the equivalent volume include the wetness of the reed and the amount of lip damping employed while the instrument is being played.

There are two simple tests to determine if the equivalent volume of the reed-plus-staple are appropriately matched to the instrument. The first involves sounding the pitch of the reed-plus-staple system while using a normal embouchure, as described previously. Since this pitch is determined by the total equivalent volume of the reed-plus-staple setup, knowing its value for a particular instrument is a quick and efficient means for determining whether the reed is performing properly for this parameter.

A second test can be employed if the joint playing frequency is in question, such as on an unfamiliar instrument. An incorrect volume size will become apparent by comparing the pitch relationship (in the fundamental register) between the notes of the left hand to the notes of the right hand. If the equivalent volume of the reed is too large, the fundamental pitches of the left-hand notes will become progressively flatter in relation to the right-hand notes as the length of usable bore is made smaller by the opening of finger holes. As the equivalent volume is brought nearer its proper size, the left-hand notes will approach their correct intervallic relationship to the pitches of the right hand. Thus, small changes in reed volume, either by embouchure change or reed adjustment, will have the greatest effect on those lower-register notes which use only a short portion of the bore.[27]

To perform this test, first check the pitch of the lowest note of the instrument (i.e., the note fingered 123 4567) with a tuning standard. Then compare this note to its octave, without changing embouchure. If the octave is wide, the equivalent volume is too small. Conversely, if the octave is narrow, the equivalent volume is too large.

One must be cautious when using this octave test to determine the appropriate reed size, however, because the results can be easily influenced by the player's embouchure and style of playing. Since embouchure tension directly affects the size of the tip opening under playing conditions, a tighter embouchure or one that uses a biting motion (the so-called hard-cushioned embouchure) will close the tip more than a looser embouchure or one that presses the reed from all sides (the soft-cushioned embouchure).[28] Because a reed with a more closed tip will behave as though its volume were smaller, it becomes apparent that a reed with an open tip will play quite differently for someone with a strong or developed embouchure than for someone with a relaxed or undeveloped embouchure. For this reason, testing a reed for octave alignment in the lower register is usually most reliable when performed more than once on separate occasions and when the embouchure is not tired, unless one is very familiar with the instrument for which the reed is being made. This helps to ensure that the conclusions drawn have not been altered by changes in the embouchure.

Besides using a tighter embouchure, an increase in breath pressure will also reduce the equivalent volume of the reed, as will decreased lip damping by stretching the lips from side to side or by moving them more toward the throat of the reed.[29] These three embouchure-controlled factors are often disregarded in reed making; nevertheless, they should always be considered as integral components of the total reed design, especially when reeds are being made for other performers.

Besides embouchure manipulations, there are, of course, several ways in which the reed itself can be adjusted to alter its equivalent volume. The most obvious is scraping the blades, as a reed with more flexible walls will have a larger equivalent volume than one with stiffer walls. The general stiffness of the blades initially is a factor of its gouge thickness and tube diameter. A thin gouge allows the use of cane directly beneath the bark. As was previously noted, this cane is less spongy than the layers below it and can be scraped thinner than the softer cane nearer the center of the tube while still retaining a high degree of transverse stiffness. The diameter of the cane tube from which the reed is made determines the amount of arch in the blade such that a smaller tube will produce a blade with more arch than a larger one. Constructing a reed from a tube with a smaller diameter, therefore, means that its tip will be more open (if it is not subsequently altered by wire tension) and that the blades will be somewhat stiffer than the blades of a reed made from a larger tube.

Thus, one can increase the equivalent volume by an overall thinning of the blades through scraping or decrease the equivalent volume by clipping off the tip or narrowing the shape. Adjusting the wires at the throat of the reed will change the crosswise tension in the blades so that flattening the throat wires is equivalent to scraping down the blades, while rounding these wires is somewhat analogous to putting wood back onto the blades.

As described previously, changing the tip opening will also change the equivalent volume of the reed. Although the natural tip opening of the reed can be regulated by the choice of cane diameter used in making the reed, Renaissance double reeds are generally constructed with a wire at the end of the blade area to help maintain the tip opening. This wire can therefore be adjusted in order to increase or decrease the equivalent volume. Also, a performer with a stronger embouchure may also want the tip to be adjusted a bit more open so that it does not become too closed during playing.

After the lower register has been properly tuned by adjusting the equivalent volume to fit the proportions of the bore, the placement of the reed resonance should be examined. This can be tested by checking the tuning and response of the first four notes of the upper register, beginning with the octave of the note fingered 123 456–. If the reed resonance is too high, the octave notes will tend to be sharp in pitch. Conversely, if the reed resonance is too low, the octave notes will tend to be flat.

Other factors must also be considered when testing for octave alignment. Since Renaissance woodwinds have no register keys for easy production of upper-register notes, the performer must rely on a combination of increased embouchure tension, breath pressure, and consequently a higher placement of the reed resonance in order to allow the overblown notes to speak. For the notes of the lower register, the upper bore modes are actually somewhat lowered from their ideal acoustic alignment under playing conditions. As the player ascends into the second register, the higher reed resonance raises these compressed resonances slightly to form a separate, aligned regime of oscillation for the upper-register note. Combined with the added stability provided by the reed resonance, the net result is the ability to attack the overblown notes without having them drift sharp.

If, after adjusting the equivalent volume of the reed for good low-note cooperation, it appears that the reed resonance is misaligned for good cooperation in the second register, further adjustments to the scrape may be necessary. Although the above-mentioned procedures for altering the equivalent volume will

Figure 1.13. Adjusting the scrape.

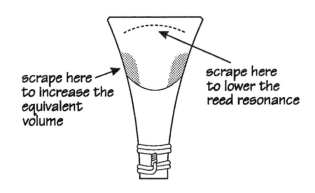

also affect the reed resonance, there are two specific areas of the reed scrape which can be adjusted in order to manipulate the reed parameters more independently. These areas are illustrated in Figure 1.13.

Since the placement of the reed resonance is highly dependent upon the width of the tip opening (distance o in Figure 1.6) under playing conditions, it can be regulated by the amount of transverse stiffness at the reed tip. Thus, to lower the reed resonance, the blades should be thinned in the area just behind the tip, as shown in Figure 1.13. If this area is scraped excessively thin, however, the reed resonance will become too flexible to stabilize the upper register properly, and register changes will be difficult or impossible. Thus, small adjustments in this area will have a large effect on the reed resonance with only a small change to the equivalent volume of the reed.

If, on the other hand, the reed resonance seems properly placed but the equivalent volume is still too small, the back and sides of the lay should be scraped, as illustrated in Figure 1.13. This action primarily affects the longitudinal stiffness of the blades. It not only increases the reed volume but also lowers the upper limit of the reed resonance. If a reasonable amount of scraping in this area does not remedy the situation, then the staple should be lengthened so that the position of the reed resonance is not compromised. If the reed resonance seems properly placed but the equivalent volume is too large, the shape can be altered by narrowing the sides of the reed blades, or the staple may need to be shortened.

As the proportions of the reed and staple fall into place, the instrument will begin to behave with typical woodwind characteristics. In general, early woodwinds of the same pitch will use a correspondingly similar length of lay, allowing for slight deviations due to the amount of taper in the blades, the gouge thickness, the size of tip opening, and personal preferences in embouchure. An instrument which seems to demand an unusual blade length may have an incorrectly sized staple, some improperly placed holes, or an atypical bore design.

Because the upper partials in the tones generated by conical woodwinds are quite prominent and lie relatively close together, an undersized reed will usually cause more unstable situations than an oversized one, because of the strong influence of the raised reed resonance. Artificially lowering the overall pitch of an instrument by enlarging its reed and staple proportions is accomplished much more easily than raising the pitch without having as many gross misalignments. For example, a small increase in the reed-plus-staple proportions will have a slight flattening effect and cause some stuffiness, whereas a small decrease in the reed parameters (away from their acoustically optimum proportions) can cause the closely spaced upper resonances to combine to form unwanted regimes of oscillation. This usually leads to greater instability, bi-stable notes, and an out-of-tune scale. Such situations can also occur if one attempts to play the instrument at a pitch level that is different from its intended tuning. Thus, when adjusting the reed for proper tuning in the various registers, one should also ascertain that the overall pitch for the fundamental register is correct by comparing it with a tuning standard.

These points are well illustrated by the instruments of the shawm family. For example, a treble shawm in D requires that the reed resonance be adjustable from about E_6 to A_6 for maximum stability. In addition, its reed-plus-staple driving frequency should be approximately A_5. In order to operate properly, the reed will therefore require a relatively short blade length with a proportionately longer staple, as shown in Figure 1.12a. If the reed is too long (as in Figure 1.12b), the lowered reed resonance will have a noticeable flattening effect on the notes of the upper register, and the instrument will feel dull, stuffy, and less stable. On the other hand, if the reed is too short, it may not be possible to adjust the reed parameters far enough through embouchure manipulation to stabilize and tune forked fingerings and upper-register notes. This will cause some notes to fly and others to have unstable or bi-stable characteristics.

In the case of the alto shawm in G, the reed resonance must have an adjustable range of about A_5 to D_6, with a reed-plus-staple driving frequency of approximately D_5. This reed requires a lower reed resonance than the treble and therefore will need longer blades. If the blades are too short, the reed parameters may be mismatched for optimum cooperation in the lower register and for good octave alignment between registers. On the other hand, if the blades are too long, upper-bore modes may be lowered too much for good cooperation, and the second-register notes will be too flat.

An interesting application of reed shape exists in the design of shawm reeds.

While many modern makers have attempted to replace these squatty, fan-shaped reeds with more straight-sided, bassoon-like ones, they do possess characteristics that help to optimize the bore design of shawms. The most obvious of these is the advantage of the wide tip for stability of low notes and cross-fingered notes. They also provide a maximum of acoustic efficiency in volume and brightness of timbre, both very desirable characteristics for instruments meant to be played outdoors.

Another characteristic, however, has to do with the interrelationship of the reed with the pirouette, especially on the treble and alto shawms. A reed with a rapidly flaring shape is extremely sensitive to the amount of lip damping by the player. This becomes very apparent when one tries to play a treble shawm without a pirouette, using a fan-shaped reed. It is actually difficult for the embouchure to remain in one place on the reed, and pitch becomes erratic. By playing the reed-plus-staple setup alone without the pirouette, it can be demonstrated that the reed-plus-staple joint playing frequency is variable by as much as a fifth (G_5 to D_6) just by moving the reed in and out of the mouth without changing breath pressure or lip tension. When the pirouette is added to the setup, it actually becomes part of the embouchure and positions the lips in their normal playing position on the reed, making the instrument feel comfortable and easily manageable. Thus, by compressing the lips against the pirouette to decrease damping, or by thickening them to increase damping, the reed parameters can be significantly altered.

This type of "lipping" is a simple technique for improving weak notes and changing registers by the sensation of a slight movement of the reed into or out of the mouth, without resorting either to biting or to relaxing the embouchure in order to make tuning adjustments. This technique also proves to be much less tiring, and by allowing a more-relaxed embouchure, it reduces the likelihood of squeaking. When playing on a fan-shaped reed, therefore, one must learn not to push the reed parameters to their upper limits, as this reduces the possibility of making further adjustments in either direction (which may be necessary for manipulating the reed parameters in order to improve the tuning or response of a note), and it greatly increases the chances for squeaking.

Types of Scrape

Probably the most widely discussed aspect of reed making is the type of scrape to use. While the characteristic timbre of an instrument is strongly influenced by the cutoff frequency of its tone holes, the reed adds a considerable amount of acoustic energy above cutoff, which contributes in a large way to the timbre by reinforcing partials that lie near its own natural resonance. The amount of acoustic energy generated in this upper region, coupled with the manner in which the player attacks and cuts off notes, determines the characteristic "sound" of a particular player and is independent of the basic acoustic requirements of the reed.[30]

How the reed generates upper partials is determined by the exact contour of the lay. A reed which emits very short puffs of air during oscillation will result in considerable production of higher harmonics and thus produce a brighter timbre.[31] The tip of such a reed closes simultaneously at the center and sides when squeezed between the thumb and first finger at the point where the lips damp the blades. Conversely, a reed which remains open over a longer portion of the cycle will generate a smaller proportion of higher harmonics and consequently produce a darker timbre. When squeezed between the fingers, this type of reed begins to close at the sides and closes last at the center. A reed which does not close completely in the center during tone production will give the darkest sound of all, to the point where a snuffling noise will be generated from the inefficient use of air unless the reed is blown very loudly. The degree of brightness can therefore be controlled in the way the tip of the reed closes.

The reed with the brightest tone is scraped evenly across the lay and tapers gradually from the back to the tip, as shown in Figure 1.14a. The reed with the darkest tone is thick along the center axis, tapering to the edges and also tapering from the back to the tip (Figure 1.14b). An even scrape is normally known as a French scrape, while a reed with a center spine is referred to as a German scrape.[32] Obviously, there are endless combinations of personal preference. Louder playing will generally increase the production of upper partials in a tone because it causes the reed tip to snap shut more uniformly. Thus, a reed with an open tip or one with a German style scrape will sound brighter and improve stability when played loudly and with high breath pressure.

The most critical part of the scrape is the region just behind the tip, indicated by the dotted line in Figure 1.14a. If the blade is too thick in this area, the tone will be dark and the reed less responsive. Since this area also controls the reed resonance, it must be scraped with care. If the blades are scraped too thin in this region, the reed will become buzzy and less stable in the lower register, while the upper register will no longer respond because the reed resonance has become either ill placed or too flexible.

Good response and the ability to attack a pitch in the overblown register are also affected by the thickness at the tip of the reed. A reed which does not respond well in the upper register is usually improved by thinning the blades at the tip and along the sides of the tip (the area above the dotted line in Figure 1.14a).

Figure 1.14. Types of scrape.

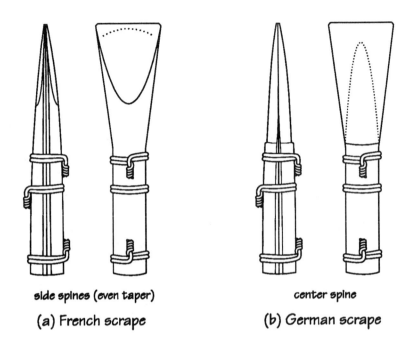

side spines (even taper)   center spine

(a) French scrape   (b) German scrape

This balancing, of course, must be carried out without disturbing the central area behind the tip.

The flatter the natural arch of the reed, the brighter the reed will be naturally, so that any scraping done in the tip area will need to be adjusted accordingly in order to achieve desired results. For example, a reed made from a small diameter of cane may need to have its blades thinned more at the center area of the tip if a bright timbre is desired. Adjustments to wires in the throat area, of course, can also alter the natural tip opening. This may in turn necessitate a change in the contour of the lay in order to retain a desired tone quality.

Most of the unevenness in the scrape can be detected by observing the tip closure. Any area that closes last is a result either of too much wood or of the cane being too stiff in that area (or in the region just behind it). Thus, balancing the area behind the tip requires that it be left thick enough to allow the upper register to be articulated easily, yet thin enough to allow good response in the lower register.

Lower-Bore Resonances

While the air-column resonances of an instrument provide it with its primary source of tonal stability, resonances in the bell sections of the shawm and curtal families serve to add further stability to important areas of the instrument. The prominence of high frequencies in the timbre of these instruments seems to be due to the nature of double-reed tone generation and the presence of the reed resonance, which lies just above the cutoff frequency of the instrument. Frequencies in this region are able to penetrate the lower bore and can excite air-column resonances of the bell section.[33] In fact, a resonance in the bell area can dramatically improve the stability of a note if it is harmonically related to the note, or it can cause the note to become erratic or unstable if the relationship is inharmonic. This is a well-known phenomenon in the curtal and bassoon families, which have an extremely long bore below the main scale. Complicated fingerings for certain notes are often utilized in order to improve stability, tone quality, and response. Even modern-day bassoonists employ some rather complicated fingerings as standard for improving the quality of certain notes on the instrument.[34]

Among all the early woodwinds, the family of shawms employs perhaps the most ingenious and sophisticated method for improving stability through the acoustics of its bell design. The treble and alto sizes were the ones most commonly employed throughout the fifteenth and sixteenth centuries. The "classic" designs of these instruments as illustrated by Praetorius[35] and found in earlier iconography are typically uniform. This suggests that these designs were worked out at a fairly early date and remained in use over a considerable period of time.[36]

The bell of the treble shawm constitutes about half the length of the instrument and contains five resonance holes. The first resonance hole is smaller than the others and is located just below the lowest finger hole. The remaining two pairs of resonance holes are located farther down, and the holes of each pair enter the bore from opposite sides, as shown in Figure 1.15a. These holes are never closed, but exist as open vent holes.

At first glance it can be seen from the spacing of the vent holes that they serve to extend the tone-hole lattice down the long bell section of the instrument for general consistency in the cutoff frequency of the tone-hole lattice and to provide for a uniform timbre by allowing all pitches to emanate from open tone holes.[37] There are in fact some other very important acoustic considerations. Figure 1.16a shows the approximate air-column resonances of the bell (with all holes closed), the successive sets of vent holes, and the lower two finger holes for a treble shawm

Figure 1.15. Hole placement on the treble shawm and alto shawm.

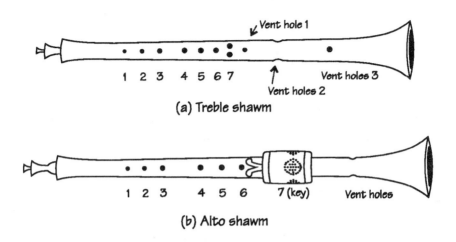

(a) Treble shawm

(b) Alto shawm

in D. Of interest to us are the bore modes which lie near the reed resonance and near the cutoff region of the tone-hole lattice. These resonances are indicated by the black noteheads in Figure 1.16a.

Notes of the lower register which contain a partial that is harmonically related to one of these bell resonances will be additionally stabilized by that section of lower bore. For example, in Figure 1.16a we see that the fifth resonance of the bell is B_5. When the pitch E_4 (fingered 123 456–) is sounded (emanating from hole 7), the fifth resonance of the bell, B_5, is also excited and contributes to the regime of oscillation for this note, adding further stability by allowing the entire length of the bore to be used. If the bell resonance B_5 is misaligned by an improper length of the bell or improper rate of bell flare, there may be an unwanted cooperation in which the mistuned B_5 could cause the fingered note E_4 to be unstable. In a similar manner, most of the lower register of the instrument is stabilized through cooperative effects with resonances in the lower bore.

An interesting part of the design of the treble shawm bell involves its ability to support both F_4 and $F\sharp_4$, using the fingering 123 45– –for $F\sharp_4$ and 123 456– with a slight relaxing of the embouchure for F_4. The note will in fact "pop" back and forth between the two distinct pitches as different parts of the bore are activated.

From Figure 1.16a we see that the bore resonances which help stabilize the note $F\sharp_4$ (fingered 123 45– –) are $F\sharp_4$, $F\sharp_5$, and $C\sharp_6$. A very stable regime of oscillation is thus possible for this note. Sounding F_4 by half-holing tone hole 6 reduces the hole size and thereby lowers its partials somewhat, but this action alone does not

Figure 1.16. Approximate resonance frequencies in the bell sections of treble, alto, and tenor shawms.

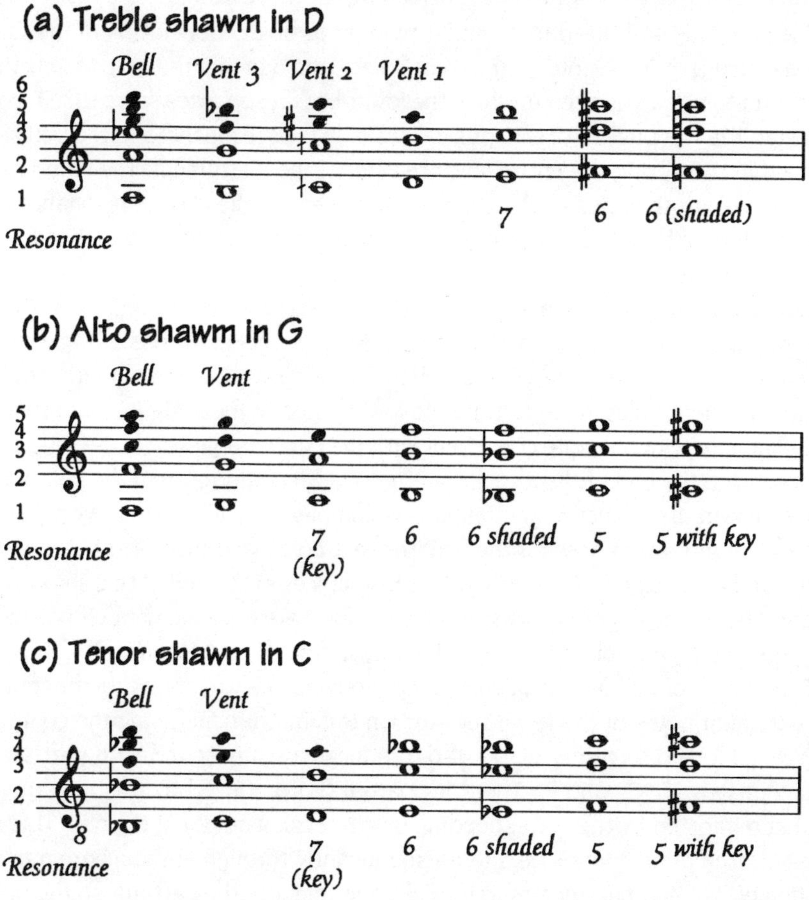

(a) Treble shawm in D

(b) Alto shawm in G

(c) Tenor shawm in C

provide accurate stability of pitch. However, by lowering the reed resonance slightly (from E_6 to approximately Eb_6) by a change in embouchure, the third partial, $C\#_6$, is also lowered. As this partial nears C_6, a cooperation occurs with the section of the bore down to the first set of double vent holes (labeled "Vent 2" in Figure 1.16a), and its own fourth resonance (C_6) is added to the regime of oscillation. This strong resonance allows the pitch of F_4 to drop a half step very accurately. Thus, accurate tuning of both the third resonance ($C\#_6$) of hole 6 and the fourth resonance (C_6) of the upper pair of vent holes (Vent 2) is necessary for the proper alignment of the regimes of oscillation needed to sound F_4 and $F\sharp_4$. Experiments confirm that the fine adjustment of these resonances can improve the playing quality of the instrument considerably for these notes.

The note F_5 is stabilized in a similar manner through cooperation of the third resonance (F_5) of the second pair of vent holes (Vent 3 in Figure 1.16a). Many other such situations can be seen in which the lower-bore resonances serve to reinforce and stabilize the pitches of the musical scale. In fact, resonances in the bell section aid in stabilizing the entire lower register of the instrument. The foundation of good design thus lies in the careful adjustment of these bore resonances in relationship to the rest of the instrument in order to offer the best overall stability and tone quality.

The bell of the alto shawm exhibits some similar acoustic properties. It is proportionally shorter than that of the treble shawm and generally has a single set of vent holes below the fontanelle, as shown in Figure 1.15b. As with the treble shawm, the vent holes serve to tune the lowest note of the scale (G_3) and to provide that note with a timbre consistent with the cutoff frequency of the tone-hole lattice. Since the bell of the alto shawm is somewhat shorter than the bell of the treble shawm, its acoustic function is less complex. The approximate pitches of the air-column resonances for the bell, the vent holes, and the finger holes of the right hand are shown in Figure 1.16b. The resonances of the bell of this shawm are in good harmonic alignment, and if the vent holes are covered, the bell produces a responsive F_3, a whole tone below the lowest note of the instrument.

This choice of bell length becomes more obvious as we look at the fingerings for particular notes of the lower register. On this instrument, using the common woodwind forked fingering of 123 4–6–produces a stuffy sound with partials of approximately B_3, C_5, and F_5. The third partial (F_5) produced by this fingering is further reinforced by the corresponding fourth resonance (F_5) of the bell. This regime of oscillation cannot be altered significantly through embouchure manipulation of the reed parameters to improve alignment of the partials, so the pitch is felt to be unsteady and dull in timbre.

When C_4 is fingered without the cross-fingering (123 4–––), we can see how the bell section is employed for its beneficial stabilizing effects. With this fingering the first three partials, C_4, C_5, and G_5, are quite well aligned. A great deal more stability is added to this combination by the cooperation of the third resonance (C_5) of the bell and especially the fourth resonance (G_5) of the vent holes. This alignment greatly improves the timbre and stability of C_4.

When C_5 is fingered 123 4–––, however, the pitch tends to fly. This happens because the note C_5 depends primarily on the reed resonance for stability. As the reed resonance is raised to C_6 by increased embouchure tension in the manner normal for overblowing, the resonance C_5 is also raised somewhat because of the change in reed parameters, and hence the resultant pitch of C_5 tends to be sharp with this fingering. By using the fingering 123 4–6–(a normal woodwind upper-register fingering), the regime of oscillation for C_5 is compromised and stabilized. This in turn allows cooperation with the resonance C_5 of the bell section, and the note is now stable and in tune.

The regimes of oscillation created by the fingerings for C_4 and C_5 are very powerful ones, but require that the player be sensitive to the placement of the reed resonance to ensure that they will operate correctly. If too small a reed is used, C_4 can in fact be pushed up to $C\#_4$ just through raising the reed resonance by biting down on the reed with one's embouchure. Thus, if the reed is adjusted incorrectly or an improper embouchure is used, unpredictable results are likely to occur. The notes C_4 and E_4 of the lower register are both particularly sensitive to the positioning of the reed resonance because of its proximity to the third partial in both regimes of oscillation (see Figure 1.5b).[38]

Another instance in which the bell section helps to stabilize an otherwise weak note is seen for the note Bb_3. The only choice of fingering available for this note is 123 456–. Hole shading alone is difficult to control very accurately, even with a wide-tipped reed. However, by receiving additional help from the prominent fourth resonance (F_5) of the bell, a more stable regime of oscillation is set up, and the note is consequently quite easily produced accurately.

The unextended tenor shawm is proportioned similarly to the alto shawm and exhibits all the same characteristics in bell design.[39] Thus, the tenor shawm in C employs a bell tuned to Bb_2 so that its third resonance (F_4) and the fourth resonance of the vent holes (C_5) provide stability for the note F_3 (fingered 123 4–––) through cooperation with the corresponding regime of oscillation. It should be pointed out that if this type of tenor shawm is played with the bell resting on a chair or on the floor, the resultant shading of the bell may alter its acoustic components and may in turn affect the regime of oscillation for the pitch F_3. The usual result is that the note will either be very unstable or will jump to near $F\#_3$. Therefore, one should always stand while playing this instrument, using a neck strap if necessary.

If the lower-bore resonances are altered or moved a distance from their optimum positions, or if the reed parameters are not properly proportioned and adjusted by the embouchure to fit the dimensions of the bore, the cooperation between bore and reed will be reduced. This may lead to undesirable results ranging from stuffy notes to extreme pitch problems. Such situations are sometimes found on instruments, and a careful analysis can often reveal how to alleviate the situation. Benade has described such adjustments as "a game that is very similar to a diagramless crossword puzzle in three dimensions."[40] Since the alignment of upper resonances as described here involves mainly the adjustment of tone hole sizes, experiments are fairly easily executed. Because some situations can become quite complex, more than one solution to a problem may be found. The final decisions regarding design must then be judged on musical grounds.

Since maximum cooperation with lower-bore resonances depends heavily upon the parameters of the reed, appropriate reed designs must be selected. A reed with a "bright" scrape will increase the participation of lower-bore resonances (and therefore improve stability in general) because of its additional production of high harmonics. Also, because the lower-bore resonances lie in close proximity to one another, the reed must have fairly stable parameters to prevent unwanted cooperations from occurring through excessive manipulation by the embouchure. If the reed volume and reed resonance are too flexible, certain notes may "jump" or seem to collapse slightly in pitch as changes in embouchure allow different parts of the bore to partake in the production of the note.

From examining the nature of the acoustics of the bell sections of shawms, it becomes clear that the desired stabilizing effects will not be optimized if these instruments are tuned in equal temperament. Because many notes must rely on harmonic relationships of the bell resonances for their stability and tuning, an approximation of just tuning is the most desirable. Quarter-comma meantone tuning (or some variation of it) provides a workable compromise and easily allows shawms enough flexibility to play the music for which they were intended with precise intonation. Meantone tuning retains the pure thirds of just intonation while slightly narrowing the fifths. Thus, for shawms pitched in G and D, the notes C♯, F♯, and G♯, in particular, must be quite low when compared to equal temperament. Table IV shows the number of cents sharp or flat from equal temperament needed to achieve meantone tuning for a selected set of pitches.

Some of the modern-day reproductions of shawms have been altered so that the cooperation with lower-bore resonances either causes intonation problems or is altogether avoided. On the smaller sizes this is easily accomplished by using an oversized reed, so that the upper resonances cannot be excited. While this sidesteps some of the problems of design and playing techniques, it also results in a rather unresonant instrument with unstable notes, a more limited range, and little subtlety. Such instruments are so different in timbre from originals that they are hardly recognizable as shawms. This poses a bit of a dilemma for the reed maker, since the best reed for these instruments may not be an acoustically optimum one. An instrument whose lower-bore resonances are well aligned over its

TABLE IV. **Quarter-comma meantone tuning adjustments for shawms and crumhorns (the number represents the distance in cents away from the note when tuned in equal temperament).**

Shawms		Crumhorns	
G	0	C	0
G♯	− 24	C♯	− 24
A	− 7	D	− 7
B	− 14	E	− 14
C	+ 3.5	F	+ 3.5
C♯	− 21	F♯	− 21
D	− 3.5	G	− 3.5
E	− 10.5	A	− 10.5
F	+ 7	B♭	+ 7
F♯	− 17.5	B	− 17.5

playing range is much less tiring to play because such a system allows the use of stiffer reeds to stabilize many notes that would otherwise need to be lipped into tune through embouchure adjustment of the reed parameters.

Crumhorn Reed Acoustics

Crumhorns and other cylindrically bored double-reed instruments are usually considered acoustically much less complicated than those with conical bores, since they do not employ an overblown register. Their similarity to the conically bored instruments, however, is much greater than might at first seem apparent. An expanding, or conical, bore may actually be thought of as a perturbation of a cylindrical one whose resonances have been compressed from a relationship of 1, 3, 5 . . . times the lowest resonance to a relationship of 1, 2, 3 . . . times the lowest resonance.[41] For example, if the cylindrical bore of a bass crumhorn in F is altered by expanding the bore until its bore modes again approach a musically useful alignment, the resultant reed and bore proportions are similar to those of an alto shawm in F, sounding an octave higher than the bass crumhorn (see Figure 1.17). Both instruments have a similar cutoff frequency and reed resonance. In the case of the bass crumhorn, however, the reed resonance lies much higher than the range of playing frequencies.

Thus, the reed resonance of a crumhorn is optimally placed just above the cutoff frequency of the bore and approximately a twelfth above the second bore reso-

Figure 1.17. Comparison of resonances in the crumhorn and the shawm.

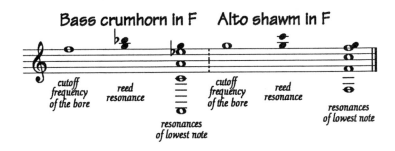

nance of the lower register note fingered Th 123 456–. This placement in turn dictates the optimum equivalent volume of the reed cavity as described previously for the conically bored instruments. After the equivalent volume of the reed cavity has been determined, the staple can then be adjusted to supply the appropriate reed-plus-staple equivalent volume required by the bore for good cooperation in the fundamental register.

Because of the relatively high placement of the reed resonance in crumhorns, alterations to it tend to have little effect on the notes of the fundamental octave. For this reason the addition of the reed and staple of the crumhorn to the top of the bore may be thought of as adding cumulative effective length to the upper end of the bore, lowering all the bore modes of a note by a nearly equal amount. Thus, the reed and staple proportions do not affect the desired harmonic relationship of the bore modes as much as they do on instruments with conical bores.

Although crumhorn staples were probably originally slightly conical, an expanding staple does not exhibit any significant acoustic difference from a cylindrical one in the fundamental octave. It does, however, allow the reed to be detachable from the staple. Since the overblown register of cylindrically bored instruments is not utilized, we need only be concerned with tone production in the fundamental register.

From our discussion of reeds for conically bored woodwinds, it follows that the parameters for adjusting the equivalent volume of the reed setup for a crumhorn are the physical size of the blades and the staple, the size of the tip opening, the motion of the reed, and the stiffness and elasticity of the cane. Performance factors which alter the equivalent volume include the wetness of the reed (if the reed is in fact meant to be wetted) and, in the case of the *Sordun* and the *Rackett*, the amount of lip damping while the instrument is being played.

Figure 1.18. Cane-to-staple proportions in crumhorns.

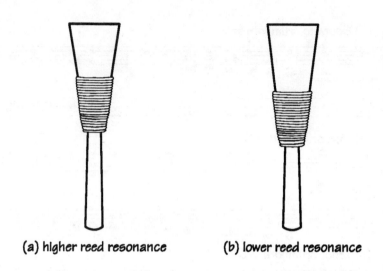

(a) higher reed resonance   **(b) lower reed resonance**

A more difficult parameter to ascertain and adjust in crumhorn reeds is the proper placement of the reed resonance. Although the crumhorn is used only in its fundamental register, the placement of the reed resonance just above the cut-off frequency of the bore will enhance stability and timbre. This concept is especially important in crumhorn reed making, because when using cylindrical staples one can erroneously make oversized or undersized blades and then correct the pitch by shortening or lengthening the staple to compensate, as illustrated in Figure 1.18. These actions will provide an appropriate equivalent volume for the instrument but can place the reed resonance in an undesirable area. Generally speaking, if the reed resonance is too low, the tone may sound duller because of the compression or suppression of upper bore modes, and cross-fingerings may be too flat or unstable. Conversely, if the reed resonance is placed too high, upper partials may at times dominate, resulting in squeaks, a brighter sound, and less effective cross-fingerings.

An improperly sized equivalent volume will have a greater effect on the left-hand notes than on the right-hand ones. Thus, if the reed volume is too large, the upper notes of the instrument will tend to be flat in relationship to the lower notes. As the proportions of the reed-plus-staple driving system are brought into alignment with the requirements of the bore, the instrument will approach correct tuning. Finding this balance is actually quite easy. For example, if the tip

Figure 1.19. Approximate resonances in crumhorns.

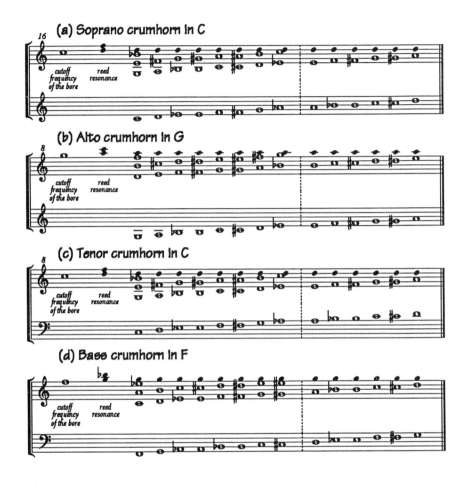

needs to be opened for improved response, the equivalent volume is also increased and the pitch of the left-hand notes will flatten. To compensate, the staple can be shortened in order to maintain the general overall pitch balance.

Figure 1.19 shows the approximate resonances for each note of the scale for soprano, alto, tenor, and bass crumhorns. The white note at the beginning of each staff indicates the approximate cutoff frequency of the instrument, while the black notes indicate the vicinity of the reed resonance for maximum cooperation with the bore. The partials in the vicinity of the reed resonance are strengthened by its presence, and this adds to the overall tone color of the instrument.

Because the player has no direct control over the reed, the equivalent volume can only be adjusted by the construction of the reed and by the player's breath pressure during playing. A reed with a closed tip and stiff blades provides the least flexibility, while a reed with an open tip and flabby blades allows the most flexibility. The reed must be flexible enough to allow tuning adjustments to weak notes to be made by subtle changes in one's breath pressure, yet stiff enough to provide stable regimes of oscillation.

If the reed walls are too flabby, the equivalent volume will be more easily influenced by the player's breath pressure, and unstable situations can occur. This is particularly noticeable in the smaller sizes of crumhorns, where small fluctuations in the reed cavity can easily become noticeable fluctuations in pitch. Attacks and cutoffs of notes can also rise or sag from the effects of the change in blowing pressure on a flabby reed.

Because the elasticity of the reed blades is sensitive to the degree of wetness, and because crumhorns and other capped reed instruments offer no direct means for embouchure manipulation, the dry reed as proposed in this manual offers some advantages for pitch stability. Reeds meant to be played without being pre-wetted must therefore be constructed a little differently from ones meant to be soaked before playing. A dry reed will thus need to be scraped more thinly than a wetted one.

All sizes of crumhorn reeds benefit from using cane obtained from tubes having as large a diameter as possible and a thicker gouge than that used for the reeds of conically bored instruments. Gouged contrabassoon cane serves this purpose well. This type of cane creates the least amount of natural arch in the reed after it has been assembled. In addition, care should be taken to keep the throat wire as flat as possible to avoid adding artificial tension to the cane. Observing these two steps will help ensure that the finished reed will be free-blowing without needing to be scraped excessively thin.

Generally speaking, a reed with a wider tip will generate more energy and produce a louder sound. The tip of a dry reed will appear very closed and the blades uniformly thin down to the top wire, with an additional wedge-shaped cut taken out of the heart, as with a bagpipe reed. Opening the tip will flatten the pitch, increase the amount of sound, and decrease stability by causing the equivalent volume of the reed to be more sensitive to breath pressure. Closing the tip will cause the reverse to happen. For example, opening the tip slightly may improve forked fingerings but have an overall flattening effect on the pitch. This in turn can be improved by shortening the staple. Tip adjustment may also be necessary to obtain a proper balance of breath pressure and control over the equivalent volume of the reed. When this balance is achieved, the instrument will immediately feel more resonant and in tune with itself. These subtle adjustments are quite easily made in order to find a balance of correct tuning, effectiveness of forked fingerings, loudness, and blowing pressure.

The shape for the dry crumhorn reed is important so that the sides of the blades do not separate after the reed has been assembled. In this situation, the best shape is a straight-sided one (see Figure 7.7). The more fanned shapes of shawm reeds and bassoon-style reeds tend to need extra tension from the wires in order to keep the blades together at the tip. This method in turn requires that the blades be scraped excessively thin in order to operate properly. The straight-sided shape thus allows for only a minimum of arch in the blades. The throat of a reed made from this shape will be quite wide and is advantageous because it adds pitch stability by minimizing the amount of pitch fluctuation that can be made through changes in breath pressure. It also reduces the ability of the reed to be overblown.

Because of the flatness of the blades and the lack of artificial tension from wires, dry reeds are very stable and will remain so as long as they are kept at constant high humidity or played every day but never actually wetted with water or saliva. A reed that has been allowed to dry out to a very low humidity can be revived by blowing gently through the instrument for several minutes. If the tip of the dried-out reed is squeezed open or shut in order to work, it may not play correctly after it has been warmed up and hence will need further adjustment.

If reeds are not being used for a period of time, they can be stored in a controlled humidity environment. Such a system is shown in Figure 1.20.[42] It consists

Figure 1.20. Controlled humidity box for reed storage.

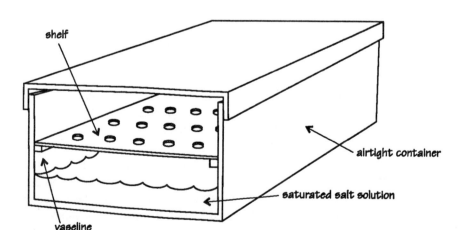

of a sealable container in which the humidity is kept constant at about 75% by a saturated sodium chloride solution. A plastic Tupperware or Rubbermaid container with an airtight cover can be used. Prepare the salt solution by adding non-iodized salt to boiling water until no more will dissolve. Apply a line of vaseline to the inside of the container just above the water line to keep the salt from creeping up. After adding the salt solution, add a few tablespoons of salt so that some undissolved salt is always present. A perforated shelf for holding reeds can then be placed inside the box so that it rests above the water. Avoid allowing any salt from the solution to contaminate the reed storage area. Crumhorn reeds that have been stored in this manner will remain in good playing shape, even if they are used only occasionally.

II

EMBOUCHURE TECHNIQUES

We are perhaps at somewhat of a disadvantage when we attempt to assess early wind techniques by applying our knowledge of twentieth-century styles of wind playing. Although the playing techniques of both ancient and modern double-reed woodwinds have much in common, the stability built into the modern oboe and bassoon by their bore designs allows the performer much liberty in embouchure formation and style of playing. Some of these techniques cannot be directly applied to the inherently less stable woodwinds of earlier times without eliciting some undesired consequences. The embouchure and manner of blowing should therefore be considered inseparable but adjustable parts of the reed-plus-staple setup, rather than inflexible factors around which the other components must be fashioned.

Among the variable components of the reed-plus-staple setup, the embouchure can exert considerable influence over the two acoustically essential parts of the reed, the equivalent volume and the reed resonance. The velocity of the air stream will also affect these components. Thus, biting the reed (i.e., vertical pressure) during playing will cause the tip to operate in a more closed state, resulting in a reduced equivalent volume and a higher reed resonance. Blowing harder through the reed or blowing with a more focused air stream will in turn cause similar effects. Conversely, less pressure on the reed blades and/or less air put through the reed will lower the reed resonance and increase the equivalent volume.

More importantly, increasing the damping of the blades (by moving the lips farther toward the tip of the reed) will increase the equivalent volume somewhat and also lower the reed resonance by a significant amount. It should be noted that adjusting the amount of reed damping by the lips is acoustically different from biting down on the reed. Biting can only raise the reed resonance or decrease the reed volume, whereas increasing or decreasing the amount of lip damping allows these parameters to be adjusted in both directions. Additionally, increased damping will limit the amount of manipulation that can be elicited by biting. In other

TABLE V. **Effects of embouchure formation on the reed resonance and the equivalent volume of the reed.**

Reed resonance raised and/or reed volume decreased	Reed resonance lowered and/or reed volume increased
1. more biting	1. less biting
2. less lip damping	2. more lip damping
3. blowing harder	3. blowing more gently

words, a subtle movement of the lips forward or back on the reed blades affords one the most control in adjusting the reed resonance or the reed volume for maximum stability and resonance for a particular note. This is an extremely important concept for playing in tune on instruments whose designs entail certain compromises which necessitate making slight adjustments to the embouchure during playing.

These embouchure variables can best be understood by actually testing them. Since we know that the lowest resonance frequency of the reed-plus-staple combination of a conically bored woodwind is constant throughout its lower register, sounding the reed with its staple can provide us with a very handy diagnostic tool. After removing the staple from the instrument to be investigated, attach the reed and blow the assembly as if it were still connected to the instrument, using the same embouchure and breath pressure. On most instruments the resultant pitch should be in the neighborhood of the octave of the note fingered 123 −−−−. After this pitch has been determined, try bending the pitch of the reed setup, using the manipulations that were just discussed. (These variables have been summarized in Table V.) Also note the degree of pitch fluctuation possible for each maneuver. This test provides an indication of the flexibility of the equivalent volume of the reed cavity.

Next, remove the reed from the staple and buzz it alone, using the same embouchure as when playing the instrument. This pitch will approximate the reed resonance under playing conditions. By adjusting your embouchure as described in Table V, you should be able to change this pitch over a range of about a fifth. (The ranges for the reed resonances of the different sizes of shawms are given in Figure 1.5.)

You will notice that each embouchure change has a simultaneous effect on both the equivalent volume and the reed resonance. In addition, the exact placement of the reed resonance can be manipulated independently from the equivalent volume by lip damping. This technique is used to improve the tone quality and stability of certain notes of the lower register as well as to stabilize the entire upper register.

With a properly designed instrument, the equivalent volume must be finely adjusted for the fundamental scale, while the reed resonance needs fine adjustment for good cooperation in the second register. A reed that needs wildly differing embouchures for the different registers is difficult to play in tune, especially if the music requires changing registers quickly. On the other hand, if a reed instrument is designed so that it needs an identical embouchure for both registers, it will be difficult to change registers smoothly without a register key. Because early woodwinds are not equipped with register keys, they must rely on this slight change of embouchure to allow upper notes to sound. Thus, when the note A_4 is played on a treble shawm in D, the reed resonance operates near E_6, as shown in Figure 1.5a. However, when the embouchure is tightened and the reed resonance is raised to A_6, the regime of oscillation that stabilized A_4 is weakened considerably, and a new and stable regime of oscillation can be formed for A_5, an octave above A_4.

We are now in a position to understand more about the effects of some of the more commonly used embouchure adjustments. For example, if the lowest notes of an instrument feel too sharp, the experienced player will instinctively either move the lips back toward the tip of the reed for increased damping of the blades or lower the jaw to allow a wider tip opening during playing. Both of these actions increase the equivalent volume of the reed and thereby lower the pitch of this note. Another situation occurs when a note is played with a *crescendo*. The increased blowing pressure causes a noticeable rise in pitch. To compensate, the embouchure is relaxed slightly to offset the change in breath pressure, and the resultant pitch remains steady.

Another important point that should be noted here is that increased lip damping effectively curtails the amount of pitch bending that can be accomplished by biting down on the reed. The modern oboe and bassoon embouchures have handled this situation in different manners. Most oboists play with only a small amount of the blades inside the mouth. The bassoonist, on the other hand, inserts the reed blades far into the mouth and usually uses an exaggerated overbite in the embouchure formation. Using such an embouchure on an oboe reed produces many sharp notes or otherwise out-of-tune notes. On the bassoon this is compensated for by the type of scrape, using a thick spine down the center of the blades (the German-style reed) or thick areas along the edges of the blades (the French-style reed[1]). Both reed types are shown in Figure 1.14. These longitudinal "spines" help to stabilize the acoustic parameters of the reed for a bassoon-style embouchure while allowing one's lower lip (via the underbite) some fine control over the damping of the bottom blade of the reed. This type of control, therefore, allows the adjustment of the acoustic parameters of the reed by the amount of damping of the lower reed blade and by adjustment of the tip opening through the powerful leverage created by the overbite. Such an embouchure is very useful for the modern bassoon, because its lowest notes must be lipped down slightly, and the reed resonance must be pushed up in order to play the highest notes of the instrument. This type of reed setup affords the greatest flexibility possible from a single driving system that must operate efficiently over the bassoon's range of some three and a half octaves.[2]

The modern oboe reed, on the other hand, employs the more evenly scraped blades of the French-style scrape and is designed to be played with less of the reed blades in the mouth.[3] Since its range is a little smaller than that of the bassoon, the oboe does not require a reed with such acoustically flexible characteristics. The increased lip damping in this driving system in turn alters the tonal character of the sound so that a darker timbre is generally preferred even though a very bright sound can be elicited from its French-style scrape through decreased lip damping. While the German-style bassoon scrape could be adapted to the oboe reed, its lack of subtlety and limited ability to control the timbre (due to playing this type of reed with much of the blade area undamped) make it a less desirable overall choice for the oboe family of instruments.

One should be cautious about using an overbite-type embouchure on early instruments, because if the reed has not been designed with a strong spine, less stable notes will tend to fly more easily.[4] Finding an appropriate embouchure for a given instrument therefore is somewhat dictated by the style of scrape. Reeds with a German-style scrape are usually meant to be played with less damping, while reeds with a French-style scrape require that the reed be more heavily damped.[5]

By observing the corresponding changes in scraping style from a heavily damped reed (such as an oboe reed) to a completely undamped reed (such as a crumhorn reed), one sees that the length of the lay must be made progressively longer in order to maintain a comparable reed resonance. Less damping decreases embouchure control of the placement of the reed resonance as well as control over timbre. Thus, there can be an infinite number of variations that lie somewhere between these two extremes of scraping styles which will in turn require a slight adjustment in the way the reed is damped by one's embouchure. The final choice of reed scrape coupled with an appropriate embouchure is then determined primarily by musical considerations.

The wind players found in artwork of the fifteenth and early sixteenth centuries are generally depicted with their cheeks puffed out while they are playing. Particularly noticeable are the shawmists of this period.[6] With their cheeks fully inflated they appear to have the corners of their mouths pressed tightly against the pirouette of the instrument. This manner of playing does not negate the use of lip damping, but does encourage the production of a bright, loud sound, which was most certainly a desired timbre for outdoor playing or for playing in large halls.[7] As was noted in Chapter I, the pirouette coupled with a fan-shaped reed also allows for a special technique of reed adjustment that permits the acoustic parameters of the reed to be manipulated while keeping the corners of the mouth near or on the pirouette. With this setup neither pinching nor the use of an overbite is necessary for subtle adjustments to the reed.

In modern double-reed embouchures the terms "soft cushion" and "hard cushion" are used primarily to describe the placement of the corners of the mouth.[8] The soft-cushion style of embouchure emphasizes a forward placement of the corners so that the lips act like a drawstring, pushing from all directions around the reed. The hard-cushion embouchure, on the other hand, requires that the corners of the mouth be pulled back into a "smile" position, stretching the lips and creating well-formed dimples in the cheeks. This type of embouchure emphasizes the biting motion of the embouchure and hence allows less control over the adjustment of the acoustic parameters of the reed.

The shawm embouchure more closely resembles the modern soft-cushion embouchure, but with the cheeks inflated. This style of embouchure can be approximated by a simple procedure. First, place your index finger into your mouth as if it were the reed setup, and then suck on it as if drawing water through a drinking straw. Your cheeks will deflate and the corners of your mouth will pull forward and inward around your finger. Your jaw should also drop down, as in the vowel sound "oh." Finally, with the corners of your mouth in this position, relax your cheeks and allow them to puff out slightly. This style of embouchure allows the player the necessary lip control combined with a freer, more open sound, and a bassoon-style overbite is not necessary. This relaxed type of embouchure is in fact useful for most early woodwinds.

Because the lower lip is usually slightly thicker than the upper lip, there exists naturally a small amount of overbite within the embouchure formation. Deliberately making this overbite more pronounced (as in the modern bassoon embouchure) when playing early woodwinds inevitably gives the player too much control over the reed parameters. The most common errors are a decreased equivalent volume caused by excessive biting as the embouchure tires, leading to sharp low notes, and, more seriously, a reed resonance that is pushed too high. This can bend upper resonances quite far out of their desired positions and may cause upper register notes to fly. It can also have disastrous effects over the entire range

Figure 2.1. Holding positions of the instrument.

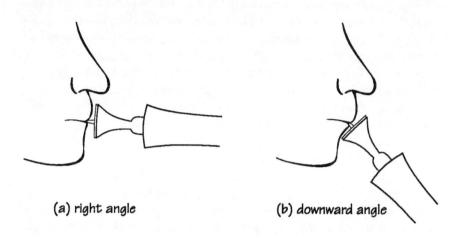

     (a) right angle   **(b) downward angle**

of the instrument on certain notes which rely upon bore resonances near the reed resonance for their proper tuning.

    The angle at which the reed enters the mouth is often overlooked by shawm players or simply carried over from their style of playing on modern instruments. A reed which enters the mouth straight on will usually produce a brighter and somewhat less "controlled" sound than one which enters the mouth at a lesser angle (see Figure 2.1), because of the change in the amount of lip damping of the upper and lower reed blades. The employment of a downward angle on a shawm (Figure 2.1b) tends to create a darker, softer tone and may cause weak notes to fly more easily because of the increased embouchure control over the reed. Thus, a brighter and more stable tone can be achieved by changing the angle of the reed to a right angle with the teeth, as shown in Figure 2.1a. This can be effected either by lowering the head slightly or raising the bell of the instrument until the proper angle is achieved.

    Although puffing the cheeks is considered detrimental to modern playing techniques, it can provide an additional parameter for regulating breath pressure when playing early instruments. Puffing the cheeks tends to make the air stream less focused and decreases its pressure on the reed. This is easily demonstrated by playing the note fingered Th 12‒ ‒‒‒‒ on a crumhorn. Starting with a "smile" embouchure (cheeks tight and the corners of the mouth pulled back) and the vowel position "ee" in the throat, sound the note. Then, while continuing to play with a constant breath pressure, puff out your cheeks by relaxing the corners of your mouth and dropping your jaw to the vowel position "oh." A slight sag in pitch will be noticeable. Using such changes in breath pressure to make subtle alterations in the behavior of the reed, as described in Table V, is a very effective method for tuning or improving weak notes without having to change one's embouchure. For crumhorns it is the only mechanism available for changing the acoustic parameters of the reed, since direct lip control is not possible on a capped reed. Thus, by maintaining a relaxed embouchure and loose cheeks as a normal playing mode, one can then influence the pitch of a note in either direction by altering the size of the air column within the mouth and throat areas.

When contemplating all the possible variations in styles of embouchure and reeds for early woodwinds, the first and foremost considerations should be musical ones. They are in fact the same musical standards to which a modern woodwind performer aspires. Thus, when the reed and the embouchure are properly adjusted, the instrument should have a desirable tone quality throughout its usable range; it should be stable and well in tune with itself; it should have at least moderate dynamic capabilities; it should be easy to articulate; and it should not be tiring to play.

Accomplishing these goals, of course, requires first of all that the instrument has been well designed. The better the resonances of the instrument are aligned, the less effort is needed by the player to sustain a pitch or push it into tune. The function of the embouchure, then, should be to allow the reed and the bore to have maximum control at all times and to intervene only for slight tuning adjustments, changing registers, and performing dynamic contrasts. The best combination for achieving this goal is a relaxed embouchure coupled with a reed that is stiff enough so that the embouchure does not bend its acoustic parameters too easily, yet flexible enough to allow proper tuning of the instrument. As there are probably as many different subtleties of embouchure as there are performers, the key here is to analyze one's own embouchure by experimenting with the reed on its staple and by itself to see what alterations will provide the greatest overall benefit.

An extremely useful exercise for developing good embouchure control is to play the harmonics for each fingering of the fundamental scale of the instrument. For example, using the fingering 123 4567 on the treble shawm in D, one can sound D_4, D_5, and A_5. (If the upper notes do not respond, try leaking an upper finger hole in order to allow the harmonic to speak. The hole can then be immediately reclosed and the harmonic brought into tune.) A chart of harmonics that should be playable on treble and alto shawms is shown in Figure 2.2. This technique can also be applied to other instruments which employ an uncapped reed.

If the harmonics are difficult to tune or unplayable, one or more of the following

Figure 2.2. Playing harmonics on the treble and alto shawms.

conditions may exist: (1) the instrument is not in tune with itself; (2) improper embouchure formation is pushing the harmonic out of alignment or making it unplayable; (3) the reed is too flabby and therefore is being too easily manipulated by the lips; or (4) the reed has an improper resonance and cannot be made to cooperate well with the bore. On the other hand, if the reed and the bore have been adjusted properly, playing harmonics in this manner will effectively aid in training the lips to adjust the reed resonance for optimum tuning and in turn will vastly improve one's upper-register playing.

III

REED-MAKING TOOLS

The tools used for reed making have changed little during the period of history for which we have documentation. Written and pictorial descriptions of reed making and associated tools first appeared in the eighteenth century. Illustrations of tools can be found in Diderot's *Encyclopédie* (1765), J. F. Garnier's *Méthode raisonnée pour le hautbois* (c. 1800), Henri Brod's *Méthode pour le hautbois* (c. 1826), Joseph Frö-lich's *Vollständige theoretisch-praktische Musikschule* (1810–11), Etienne Ozi's *Nouvelle méthode de basson* (1803), and Carl Almenraeder's *Die Kunst des Fagottblasens* (c. 1842).[1] These tools are all similar to those used today, except for the fact that hand gouging has largely been replaced by machine gouging. Although these sources are all admittedly quite late, they do indicate that while the tonal preferences and bore designs of instruments have changed significantly over the last 250 years, the basic methods for working with *Arundo donax* have not.

Anyone experienced in reed making for the modern oboe or bassoon already possesses most of the necessary equipment for making Renaissance double reeds, except perhaps for the tools needed for hand gouging and some smaller mandrels for making shawm reeds. The tools discussed in this chapter fall into three categories: (1) tools necessary for adjusting a finished reed (shown in Figure 3.7), (2) additional tools and materials required for constructing a reed, and (3) tools that are recommended but optional, depending on one's particular needs (Figure 3.8). Most of these tools can be purchased from a double-reed supply house or improvised from common hardware store tools.

Tools Used for Reed Adjustment

Scraping knife: A high quality knife designed for scraping the cane is a prerequisite for reed making and for subsequent adjustments after the reed has been made. This knife should have a bevel-edged, rigid blade of tempered steel (see Figure 3.9a). It is sharpened to retain a slight J-shaped wire edge. For this reason,

Figure 3.1. Reed-making tools. D. Diderot and J. le Rond d'Alembert, *Encyclopédie* (Paris, 1765). *Receuil de Planches*, Volume V: Lutherie, Plate X.

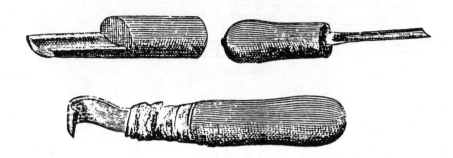

Figure 3.2. Reed-making tools. Joseph François Garnier, *Methode raisonnée pour le hautbois* (Paris: Pleyel, *c.* 1800).

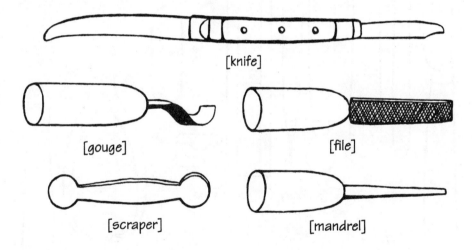

it is used for scraping in one direction only, and right- and left-handed models are available. To avoid damaging the edge, never use it for tasks other than scraping the reed.

Cutting knife: The cutting knife is a utility knife used for such tasks as cutting pieces of cane to proper length, profiling, shaping, and trimming the tip of the reed. This knife is hollow ground (see Figure 3.9b) and honed to a razor-sharp straight edge. It is thus sharpened differently from the scraping knife. Both knives

Figure 3.3. Reed-making tools. Henri Brod, *Méthode pour le hautbois* (Paris: c. 1826).

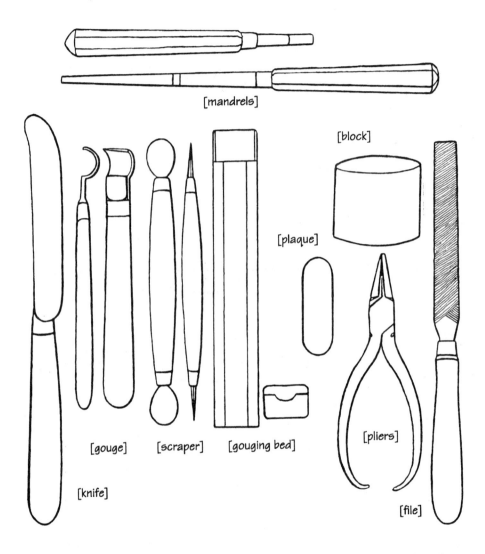

[mandrels]

[block]

[plaque]

[gouge]   [scraper]   [gouging bed]

[pliers]

[knife]

[file]

should always be stored in a protective (preferably leather) case so that their edges do not become nicked. (Instructions for sharpening both types of knives are found at the end of this chapter.)

Cutting block: The cutting block is a small piece of hardwood or plastic with a slightly convex surface, on which the reed is placed when trimming the tip with a knife or a razor blade. The block should be made from a dense material so that the

Figure 3.4. Reed-making tools. Joseph Frölich, *Vollständige theoretisch-praktische Musikschule* (Bonn, 1810–11).

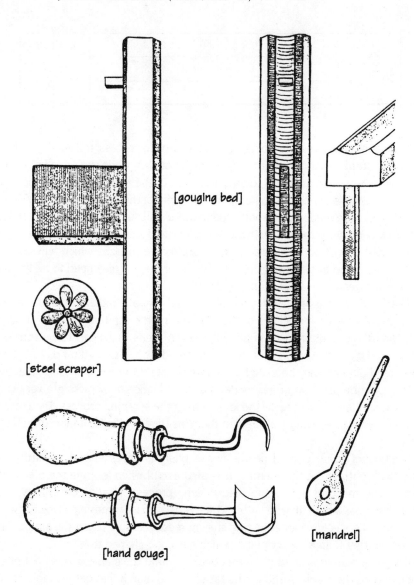

Figure 3.5. Gouging bed. Etienne Ozi, *Nouvelle methode de basson* (Paris, 1803).

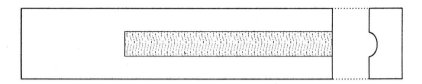

knife does not compress its fibers during the cutting process. It also should have a slip-resistant surface so that the reed does not shift while the tip is being cut.

Mandrel: Mandrels are used to form the tube of the reed and to hold the reed while it is being scraped. It should match the taper of the staple or bocal for which the reed is being made. A bassoon-reed mandrel will suffice for many reed styles. For shawm reeds, scratch awls make excellent and inexpensive mandrels. They can be obtained from a hardware store and come in sizes which will usually match treble and alto shawm staples. The tip of the awl may need to be ground down if it extends too far into the reed.[2]

Plaque: The plaque is a thin piece of material (usually metal or plastic) which is inserted between the blades of the reed during the scraping process. It helps to support the blade and to point out uneven areas that need to be thinned. Oboe-reed plaques work well for the smaller reeds, while thin guitar picks or bassoon-reed plaques may be used for the larger sizes. Contoured bassoon plaques should only be used on larger reeds, if at all. Plastic guitar picks are very economical and less damaging to the knife during the scraping process. Try to avoid the ones with advertising stamped on them, as they tend to be lumpy around the lettering.

Needle-nosed pliers: A small needle-nosed pliers is necessary for adjusting the wire that controls the tip opening. It is also useful when forming the reed tube around the mandrel during the reed-making process. In addition, this type of pliers often has a built-in wire cutter, which is needed for trimming off excess wire. A jewelry pliers is ideal for adjusting shawm reeds. Be sure to get the kind with a flat grip rather than a rosary pliers, which has cone-shaped tips.

Reamer: A reamer is used if the reed leaks around the staple or does not fit far enough onto the staple. Although its taper should match that of the staple or bocal, a bassoon reamer will usually suffice for most reeds. For smaller reed sizes a round needle file can be used.

Sandpaper: Wet-or-dry sandpaper is a good substitute for Dutch rush and is

Figure 3.6. Reed-making tools: (1) gouging bed, (2) hand gouge, (3) scraper, (4) mandrel, (5) pliers. Carl Almenraeder, *Die Kunst des Fagottblasens* (Mainz, c. 1842).

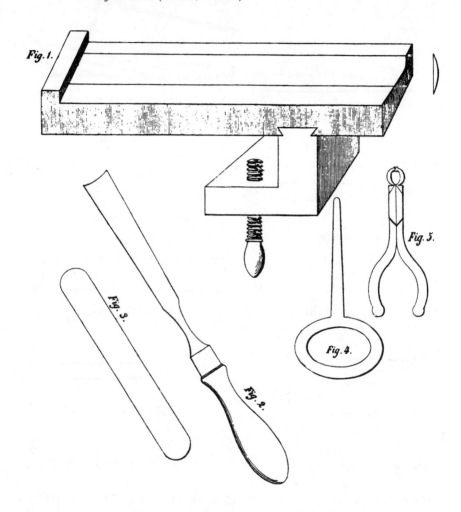

used for making fine adjustments and for the final polishing of the lay. The recommended sizes are #320 for removing wood and #600 for polishing.

Oilstone: A fine-grade stone is necessary for keeping the knives sharp. Because of the relatively high silica content of *Arundo donax*, the scraping process quickly dulls the edge of the knife. Scraping with a dull knife generally leads to the tearing and flattening of the cane fibers along with excessive downward pressure, which

Figure 3.7. Tools for reed adjustment.

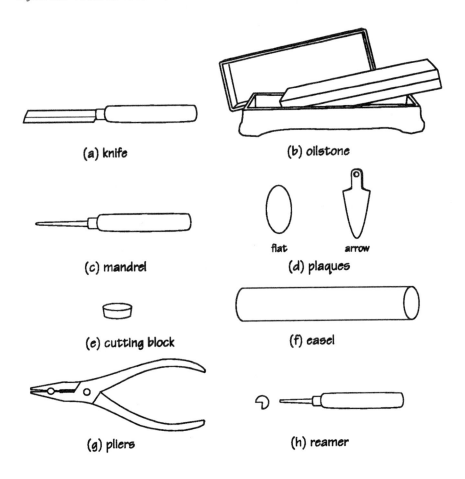

(a) knife

(b) oilstone

(c) mandrel

flat   arrow

(d) plaques

(e) cutting block

(f) easel

(g) pliers

(h) reamer

may cause the blades to crack. A 6″ × 2″ stone is the easiest to work with to obtain a uniform edge on the knife.

There are many types of natural and synthetic stones available. Arkansas natural stones can be obtained in four grades: Washita (coarse), Soft Arkansas (medium), Hard Arkansas (fine), and Black Hard Arkansas (extra fine). A light oil such as mineral oil or 3-*in*-1 oil is used as a lubricant during sharpening so that the stone does not become damaged. Japanese waterstones have also become popular. Because they are lubricated with water rather than oil, cleanup is easier. Arkansas stones can also be lubricated with water if necessary. Synthetic stones include aluminum oxide (India, Alundum), silicon carbide (Carborundum, Crys-

Figure 3.8. Optional tools.

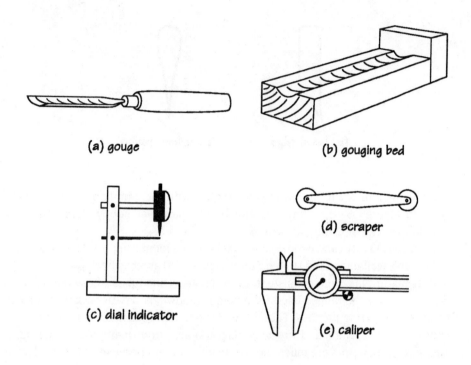

(a) gouge   (b) gouging bed

(c) dial indicator

(d) scraper

(e) caliper

tolon), and diamond. A Soft Arkansas stone is a good all-around choice for sharpening reed knives. If used properly, it will last indefinitely.

Additional Tools and Materials for Reed Making

Binding materials: Standard bassoon reed supplies work fine for reed assembly. #22 soft brass wire is appropriate for most reeds, whereas #24 brass wire may be preferable for treble shawm reeds because of their small size. #20 brass wire may be used on very large reeds. Nylon string and waterproof glue such as *Duco Cement* provides a durable and long-lasting binding. These materials are available from a double-reed supply house or a hardware store.

Brass tubing and tubing cutter: Brass tubing may be required for making new staples for crumhorn reeds. (If your crumhorns have conical staples, then new tubing is not necessary.) The cutter is needed for adjusting staples to the proper length. A different diameter of tubing should be used for each size of crumhorn. (Appro-

Figure 3.9. Reed knives.

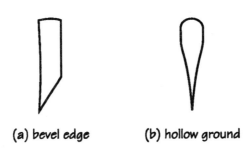

(a) bevel edge   (b) hollow ground

priate diameters of tubing have been supplied with the crumhorn reed dimensions in Figure 7.3.) Brass tubing can be purchased at hobby stores and is available in one- or three-foot lengths.

Cane: Top-quality cane is obviously a prerequisite for making good reeds. Most of the cane available in the United States is imported and has been presorted so that its maturity is quite consistent. Unfortunately, cane tubes whose diameters do not fall into the ranges used for modern woodwinds are discarded at some point in the sorting process. Tubes used for bassoon reeds have a diameter of approximately 25 mm and are generally available from mail-order suppliers. Tubes larger than this are much more difficult to obtain because not as much of the cane grows to this size, and the tubes that are harvested are saved for producing gouged contra-bassoon cane or single reeds. This is unfortunate since many of the larger Renaissance-reed styles benefit from being fashioned from tubes of a larger diameter. For these reeds gouged contrabassoon cane should be used, though it is more expensive. *Arundo donax* does grow naturally in California and some other areas of the country and may be worth harvesting for this purpose. If cane and reed-making supplies are unavailable locally, they may be purchased directly from one of the suppliers listed in the Appendix.

Easel: The easel supports the cane during profiling and measuring. The bed area of a commercial oboe or bassoon easel is recessed to help hold the cane in place. Since most Renaissance reeds can be made from bassoon cane, a modern bassoon easel may be used. An inexpensive alternative is to cut a length (five or six inches) of one-inch diameter wooden or plastic dowel.

Flat-tip pliers: A flat-tip pliers is needed for drawing the wires tight during reed construction. A needle-nosed pliers is not a good choice for this task because the tip is not wide enough to get a firm grasp on the wires.

Ruler: A small metric ruler for measuring the cane will suffice. Since both the English and the metric systems are still used, a pocket calculator should be available for making any necessary conversions, remembering that 1 inch = 25.4 millimeters and 1 millimeter = .03937 inches.

Wire cutters: If your pliers does not have them built-in, then a separate pair of wire cutters will be necessary for trimming off excess wire.

Optional Tools and Materials

Beeswax: Beeswax has a variety of uses, from adjusting tone holes for tuning purposes to fixing the seal between the reed tube and its staple. It is available from a double-reed supply house.

Caliper: While a small ruler is adequate for most measuring needs, some prefer using a dial or vernier caliper. A caliper is especially useful for copying the dimensions of an old reed.

Cyanoacrylate glue: Krazy glue can extend the life of a cracked reed or be used to make an emergency repair to a reed. Insert a very small amount into the crack and hold the cracked area together and flush until the glue dries. Be sure the cracked sides of the blades are horizontally aligned at the tip so that a proper tip closing under playing conditions is preserved. The reed may behave differently because of the stiffness of the glued area. To minimize this, sand off any excess glue or scrape lightly over the glued area.

Dial indicator: A dial indicator (dial micrometer, dial gauge) is a measuring instrument for determining the thickness of the cane during the gouging process. Some designs also enable one to measure the thickness of the blades at various points on a finished reed. Double-reed supply houses often stock either handheld or table models. They can usually be obtained more cheaply from a company that specializes in scientific instruments.

Files: Small flat files may be used as an alternative to knife scraping and for smoothing bumps in the lay left by the scraping knife.

Gouge: There are two types of gouge that can be used for gouging cane by hand. The most common is a straight hand gouge, which has the bevel ground on the outside. The other type is the in-cannel firmer gouge (also called a back-bevel gouge), which has the bevel ground on the inside. The latter leaves a smoother surface but requires a special round-edge slipstone for sharpening. The curvature of the gouge should be equal to or greater than the curvature of the cane being gouged. I have found that using a gouge that is slightly smaller (one with a greater curvature) than the cane diameter allows for some flexibility in experimenting with different tube sizes and gouge thicknesses without needing to buy extra tools.

Gouging bed: The gouging bed is used to hold the cane in place during hand gouging. It can be fashioned from a block of wood, as shown in Figure 3.8b. The bed is formed with the gouging tool, and then an end-piece is attached to hold the piece of cane in place. The bed must match the curvature of the cane to be gouged. If you plan to gouge both bassoon and contrabassoon cane, two different beds need to be made. A C-clamp can be used to secure the gouging bed to the work table.

Saw: A small saw, such as a coping saw or a dovetail saw, may be necessary for cutting cane tubes to length.

Scissors: I find a scissors to be the most efficient method for trimming a reed tip (perhaps because I was originally taught to use this method). The scissors must be sharp and must not be used for other tasks, such as cutting wire. If you wish to try this method, I suggest practicing first on some heavy cloth to learn how to cut without letting the material bind between the blades of the scissors. After you have mastered this, experiment on some old reeds before going at your current favorite. This method may cause blades constructed from very thinly gouged cane to crack more easily during the trimming process.

Scraper: A scraper is a circular piece of fine-grade steel used for smoothing the inside of the cane after gouging and for thinning areas of the gouge where necessary. Modern gouging machines have all but eliminated the use of scrapers in modern reed making, so one must have them specially made. For general smoothing of the cane after gouging, a simple work-around is to use a piece of wet-or-dry sandpaper wrapped around a dowel of the appropriate size. For thinning areas of the blade from the inside, an English horn scraper can be used. Its diameter is too small for bassoon cane, but it is somewhat easier to control than a gouge when working on a small area. Woodworkers' molding scrapers of an appropriate size can sometimes also be obtained for this purpose.

X-acto knife: Some prefer trimming the reed tip with a single-edged razor blade or an *X-acto* knife because the blade is very thin and will cut through the cane fibers more easily without compressing them. An *X-acto* knife is also useful when using metal shapers, particularly for fan-shaped reeds, where the blade must cut across the grain at a greater angle.

Sharpening Knives

To sharpen the bevel-edged scraping knife, obtain a Soft Arkansas oilstone or other comparable stone. Place a few drops of oil (or water) on the stone for lubrication. If the stone is not well anchored to a table, place it on a damp towel to keep it from slipping while the knife is being sharpened. Holding the knife handle with the right hand,[3] place the bevel of the blade flat on the right-hand side of the near

Figure 3.10. Sharpening the scraping knife.

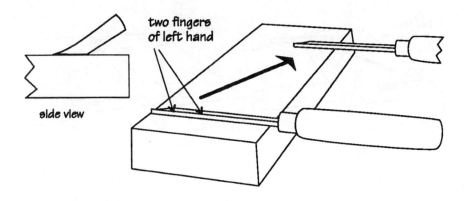

end of the stone, as shown in Figure 3.10. Place two fingers of your left hand on the knife blade toward the back to stabilize and guide the blade. Then push the blade firmly and evenly across the stone diagonally from left to right, so that the entire length of the blade is exposed to the surface of the stone (following the arrow in Figure 3.10).

To repeat the procedure, lift the blade and reset it to the original position. In order to obtain the right amount of downward pressure on the blade, imagine that you are pushing a thin slice off the top of the stone with each pass. Three or four of these strokes should suffice to restore the wire edge to the knife. After you have finished sharpening the knife, be sure to clean the stone by wiping off the oil, or, if you have used water for the lubricant, clean the stone under running water.

The hollow-ground utility knife is sharpened in a similar manner, except that passes need to be made on both sides of the blade to avoid forming a J-shaped wire edge. Holding the knife handle with the right hand, place the knife blade flat on the stone with the sharp side of the blade pointing away from you, as shown in Figure 3.11. Raise the back, thick side of the blade slightly so that the edge forms approximately a 20° angle with the stone. Then place two fingers of your left hand on the knife blade toward the back, to stabilize it, and push the blade firmly and evenly across the stone diagonally from left to right, so that the entire length of the blade is exposed to the surface of the stone (following the arrow in Figure 3.11a). At the far end of the stone turn the blade over and reposition it as far left as possible. Then raise the blade so that it forms about a 20° angle with the stone, stabilize the blade with two fingers of the left hand, and pull the knife toward you from left to right. Again, to obtain the right amount of downward pressure on the blade, imagine that with each pass you are alternately pushing and pulling a thin

Figure 3.11. Sharpening the utility knife.

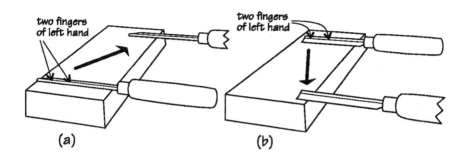

slice off the top of the stone. Each stroke back will form an "x" with the stroke forward, as shown by the arrows in Figure 3.11. Make an equal number of passes in this manner alternately on each side of the blade. When you are finished, wipe the excess oil from the stone, or, if you used water, clean the stone under running water.

Reed Cleaning and Storage

After a period of use, a reed may accumulate slimy deposits on the inside of its blades. Its responsiveness will usually be improved by a cleaning. This can be done by holding the reed under a stream of running water. Some prefer using peroxide, especially for reviving a very old reed.

Ultrasonic cleaning devices, such as those sold for jewelry cleaning, have also gained favor in recent years. Be sure to place the reed in water rather than in jewelry-cleaning solution.

Another method of cleaning is to place the corner of a crisp dollar bill between the blades; then pull it out while pressing lightly on the ends of the reed blades with your thumb and first finger. If a small particle has become lodged in the reed, it can usually be loosened by carefully nudging with a feather or a pipe cleaner from the butt end of the reed.

Proper reed storage is probably the most overlooked part of reed care. Reeds often turn black because they have not been allowed to air-dry properly. A reed case must allow adequate ventilation, so one should avoid sealable plastic containers. Cases designed for modern oboe and bassoon reeds can be used, or one can be fashioned from a small container by drilling holes in both sides to allow the moisture in the reeds to escape.

IV

CONSTRUCTING A DOUBLE REED

The guidelines for constructing a double reed can be summarized by the following procedures:

1. Selecting the cane
2. Gouging
3. Profiling
4. Folding
5. Shaping
5. Forming the tube
6. Binding
7. Opening the tip
8. Scraping

All these operations are familiar to modern double-reed players who make their own reeds. In this chapter, each step will be discussed in detail as it pertains to reed making for Renaissance woodwinds.

Types of Construction

There are two basic styles of construction used for making Renaissance double reeds. The first is the lip-controlled reed that is detachable from its staple or bocal, such as shawm and curtal reeds. The second is the type of reed used by the capped woodwinds, such as crumhorns and capped shawms. Both are depicted in Figure 4.1.

Of the lip-controlled reeds, shawm reeds are distinctive in that they have a short base and a pronounced fanned shape for use with a pirouette. Reeds for the curtal, *Sordun*, and *Rackett*, on the other hand, are usually made with a longer base (or tube) and are more similar in proportions to a modern bassoon reed. Con-

Figure 4.1. Types of double-reed tone generators.

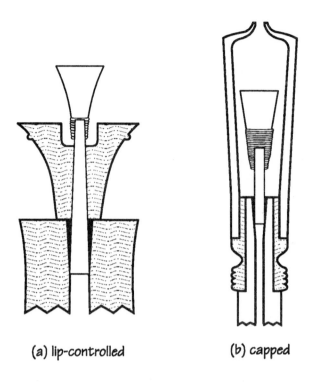

(a) lip-controlled   (b) capped

struction for the short- and the long-base reed is similar in that both are formed on a mandrel and scraped in a manner that requires the blades to be wetted and to be damped by the lips during playing for proper operation.

Crumhorns comprise the main group of capped double reeds. Relatives of this cylindrically bored family possess a similar reed setup. During the Renaissance, crumhorn reeds were probably not bound to their staples, as is commonly done today, but were placed on conical staples. Since there is no acoustic significance in using a conical staple rather than a cylindrical one on the cylindrically bored crumhorn, binding or not binding the reed to its staple is a matter of personal preference.

Capped shawms, such as the *Rauschpfeife* and the *hautbois de Poitou*, couple a capped-reed setup to a conical bore. In this situation the reed should be made separately and placed on a conical staple.

Capped reeds are scraped to operate without any lip damping. The choice remains as to whether they should be wetted first or played dry. After working with both types, I prefer dry reeds because of their stability and their relatively maintenance-free characteristics. Working with dry reeds is discussed in greater detail in Chapter 7.

The procedures described in the remainder of this chapter consist of the general techniques that apply to the basic construction of both capped and uncapped reeds. Details of scrape and specific problems according to reed type are dealt with individually in Chapters 5–8.

Selecting the Cane

Modern bassoon cane is available from suppliers in several forms: (1) tubes, (2) gouged, (3) gouged and shaped, or (4) gouged, shaped, and profiled. The first two kinds, tubes and gouged cane, can be used for early reeds. Shaped bassoon cane is too narrow for most purposes, and profiled bassoon cane is usually too thin. One exception is bassoon cane that has a very wide shape and a thick profile in order to give the reed maker greater flexibility.[1] This cane is easy to use and suitable for many reed sizes. Its chief disadvantage is that one cannot control the thickness of the gouge since it has already been profiled.

Cane that has not properly matured for use in reed making may have a greenish cast. It should be left out to air (preferably near a window so that sunlight can reach it) until it turns a golden brown. Cane with black areas or specks in the grain has been subjected to growths of mold. Since mold at this stage will usually damage the cane fibers, such cane will make poor reeds and should be discarded.

After new cane has been gouged, it should be soaked in water for 24 hours or so, allowed to dry out, resoaked for 24 hours, and again allowed to dry. Change the water between soakings, as residue within the cane will be leached out during this process. Cane that has undergone this procedure tends to be more stable and predictable during the construction process, and the finished reed usually requires less break-in time.[2] Do not leave cane in water for longer than two days at a time, because long soaking encourages the growth of mold or algae, which can render the cane unusable. Cane that is to be worked on need only be soaked for an hour or two. If the cane becomes water-logged, the fibers cannot be cut very easily with a knife or a gouge, and its swollen state will make measurements inaccurate after it shrinks back to its normal size.[3] Cane that has been profiled by machine should never be soaked for too long a period before the reed is constructed, because the hinge at the center will be weakened and the blades may break apart when the cane is folded in half.

The diameter of the cane tube used for making a reed will affect the amount of arch in the blades and the size of the tip opening. Cane taken from a larger diameter tube will cause the natural tip opening of the reed to be less arched. Conversely, using a smaller diameter tube will make the tip more open. Cane is much stronger lengthwise, with the grain, than across the grain. An excessive natural arch will add crosswise tension (and strength) to the blades, something that is not necessarily desirable if the blades need to be unnecessarily thin to compensate. Thus, although the top wire on the reed is ultimately used to control the size of the tip opening, one should aim toward using cane that follows the natural arch of the finished reed as closely as possible.

Because we basically have only the choice between using bassoon cane or contrabassoon cane for a particular type of reed, compromises are necessary. Wetted reeds, such as shawm reeds, can be made from either bassoon cane or contrabassoon cane. Larger sizes of reeds are generally better if made from contrabassoon cane.

On the other hand, capped reeds, which are meant to be played dry, such as crumhorn reeds, benefit most from using the largest diameter of cane possible. Since dry cane is much stiffer than a similar piece of wetted cane, the purpose here is to add as little additional crosswise tension as possible through the natural curvature of the blades or the placement of the wires. The dry blades can then be left proportionately thicker, and by not having excess artificial tension added to them, they will be less susceptible to warping while they are being played. This principle is less critical on wetted, lip-damped reeds but nevertheless still an important consideration.

Gouging

Hand gouging provides a simple but important method for controlling the relative stiffness of the cane from which the reed blades will be fashioned. The toughest, most resilient cane is found just below the bark. Thus, the blades of a reed made from more thinly gouged cane will utilize more of this part of the cane than if the reed were made from cane having a thicker gouge. This resilient layer of cane below the bark provides a better balance between stiffness and flexibility for early double reeds than does the spongier material farther toward the middle of the cane tube. Working with this area of the cane allows one to make reeds that are free-blowing yet possess the crosswise stiffness required for stability that could only otherwise be obtained by a reed with thicker blades. Multiple tonguings (such as double tonguing) are also more easily executed on reeds that have been constructed from thinly gouged cane.

Modern bassoon cane is usually gouged to a thickness of about 1.3 mm (.050″),[4] while contrabassoon cane is gouged to a thickness of about 1.5 mm (.060″). Eighteenth-century writers preferred a gouge somewhat thinner than this. Ozi, for example, suggested a gouge of one half *ligne* (about 1.1 mm, or .044″) for bassoon reeds, and Brod recommended a gouge of 0.75 mm (.030″) for oboe reeds.[5] Surviving eighteenth-century reeds also suggest that a thinner gouge was preferred.[6] While these sources are of a rather late date, eighteenth-century instruments are much more similar acoustically to instruments of the Renaissance than are modern ones. There is a greater need for using a reed constructed from thinly gouged cane on early instruments than on modern instruments because of the added stability such a reed provides.

If the cane is gouged too thinly, the upper partials may become too pronounced and the tone will become more strident. Also, very thinly gouged reeds crack more easily, and the tube is more difficult to make. One method used during the eighteenth century was to leave the overall gouge thicker but to scrape it thinner in the area of the blades.[7] Thus, the tube of the reed will have thicker walls, but the blades can still be fashioned from the stiffer cane just below the bark.

All cane varies in density according to its growing conditions and curing process. The greatest variation occurs in the spongy layers occurring increasingly toward the middle of the cane tube. In modern reeds, the use of a thicker gouge means that more of this spongy layer is used in the blade construction, and there are more likely to be variations in the quality of reeds, especially ones made from different batches of cane. The spongier cane produces a better timbre on modern instruments, however, and is thus still desirable for this purpose. Using a thinner gouge reduces the variation in hardness that occurs naturally in cane because the area under the bark is the most uniform area from piece to piece.

For hand gouging you will need a gouging bed and a hand gouge, as illustrated in Figure 3.8. Begin by sawing the tube of cane to the proper length, and then split it lengthwise. (This procedure can be done before the cane is soaked.) Using a utility knife or an X-*acto* knife, work the blade into the end of the grain and allow the tube to split down its length. Divide the tube in this manner into three or four pieces, depending on the width of the reed being made. The cane will split very easily along the grain, so take precaution when using a knife for this procedure. Commercial tube splitters are available from double-reed supply houses and can split a bassoon tube into either three or four sections.

Soak the cane until it is saturated (about one or two hours). Clamp the gouging bed to a table and place the cane on the bed. Using a very sharp gouging tool of a diameter similar to the cane, make a thin, continuous cut, moving toward the raised end of the gouging bed, as shown in Figure 4.2. This constant pressure should hold the cane in place, or pressure may be exerted by placing a finger on

Figure 4.2. Gouging the cane.

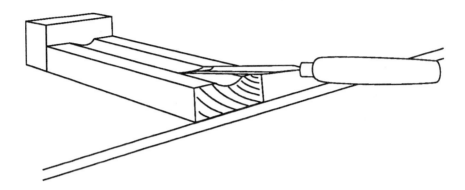

the near end of the cane to help stabilize it. Allow the gouge to follow the grain, turning the cane lengthwise between passes to maintain uniform thickness.

A dial indicator can be used to measure the cane thickness and to find uneven areas. An outside calipers set to the correct gouge thickness can also be used to test for overall thickness. After you have gouged a few pieces of cane, you will quickly develop a sense of the thickness of the cane without needing to measure it repeatedly. The age-old methods of twisting the ends with the fingers and holding the cane up to a strong light in order to check the gouge thickness are also effective and save a lot of time.

Cane tends to take the edge off tools easily, so be sure to sharpen the gouging tool often. This will allow it to follow the grain of the wood, and the result will be a smoother, more even gouge.

After gouging the cane to the desired thickness, smooth the inside of the cane with a piece of #600 wet-or-dry sandpaper wrapped around a dowel of appropriate size. Allow the cane to dry and sand it again as a final polish. If you have a scraper, it may be used for this purpose as well. A scraper usually works better if the cane is dry.

At this point you may want to thin the gouge in the area of the blades with a scraper. Measure and mark this area, and then scrape toward the center line of the cane so that the thinnest part lies in the area where the cane will be folded in half. Thinning the gouge in this manner means that, among other things, less wood will have to be removed from the outside of the blades during the final scraping of the reed. After you have completed the gouging and scraping procedures, the cane should be alternately soaked and dried twice, as described above, before it is worked on further.

If you are using gouged bassoon or contrabassoon cane, its gouge thickness can easily be thinned down by using a hand gouge and a gouging bed in the manner described above. In this situation not much additional wood will need to be removed, so the procedure will require very little extra time.

Gouging can also be done with a machine in the same manner that modern bassoon cane is gouged. However, a different bed and blade are needed for each type of reed being made. With practice, hand gouging can be done as quickly and as accurately. This allows one to experiment easily with different thicknesses and diameters of cane and ultimately gives one much greater control over critical reed parameters.

Profiling

The profiling procedure involves first removing bark from the blade areas of the gouged cane and then thinning and tapering the blades so that the cane can be folded in the middle. Begin by soaking the gouged cane for an hour or so to minimize the possibility of splitting during these next operations. Place the cane on an easel, mark the center of the cane with a pencil, and score the bark at the center with a utility knife or a single-edged razor blade. Measure the length of the area to be profiled on either side of the center and mark it with a pencil. If you have used a thin gouge or have scraped the blades from the inside of the tube as described above in the gouging process, you will need to remove only a small area of bark on either side of the center mark, as illustrated in Figure 4.3.

The lay of the reed is the length of the blade area from which bark will be removed. On a finished reed it is the distance from the tip to a point usually near the first wire, depending on the thickness of the gouge. With the utility knife carefully take off the bark with a paring motion, being careful not to cut in too deeply. Try to take very thin cuts and allow the knife blade to follow the grain. If the center line disappears, you may have to remeasure and rescore it, taking care not to cut completely through the wood. The cane should be about 0.25 mm (.010″) thick at the center line. This score forms the hinge which will hold the blades together while the tube is being formed.

If you are making a reed from cane with a standard gouge thickness, such as gouged bassoon cane, score the bark at both ends of the lay (see Figure 4.4). Remove all the bark between the scores, as shown in Figure 4.5, but do not cut into the next layer of cane too deeply. Remeasure the center of the cane, and make another score. The center mark will probably need to be measured several times and rescored as the profiling process removes it. (Another method is to mark the easel, making sure the cane is not allowed to shift. The center is then easily rescored

Figure 4.3. Adjusting the length of the lay.

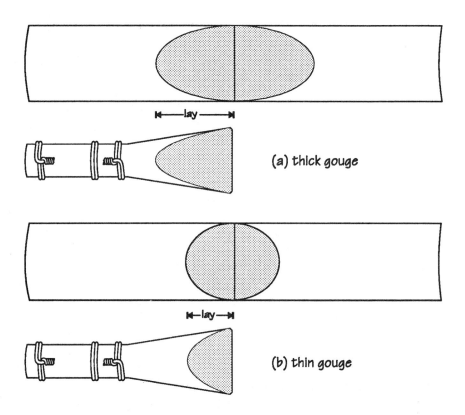

(a) thick gouge

(b) thin gouge

by following this pre-marked line.) Next, with the utility knife taper the lay toward the center mark until the cane is about 0.25 mm (.010″) across the center. This must be done from both directions toward the center line. A flat file may also be used for profiling, as shown in Figure 4.6.

Shaping

Shaping the gouged and profiled cane involves removing excess cane from the sides until the desired shape of the blades is obtained. Modern reed makers use one of two styles of tools for hand shaping (see Figure 4.7). With the standard shaper the profiled cane is folded, placed over the tip of the shaper, and secured with adjustable jaws. A utility knife is then used to trim the sides of the cane, fol-

Figure 4.4. Scoring the bark.

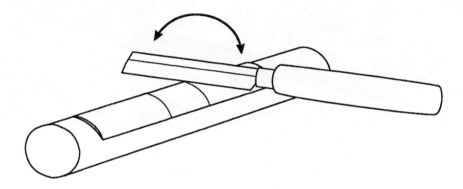

Figure 4.5. Removing the bark.

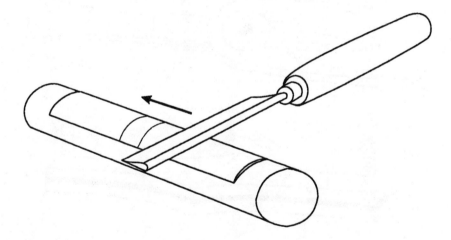

lowing the metal shape as a guide. With the straightline shaper, the cane is clamped into the shaper without being folded, and excess cane is removed along the sides with a utility knife. After it has been trimmed to the exact size of the shaper, it is removed from the device and folded.

Although these shapers are easy to use and produce uniform reeds, a modern bassoon shape is not ideal for most Renaissance reed styles. Hand shaping without the aid of a metal shaper is easy (and, in fact, was a standard procedure in

Figure 4.6. Filing the cane.

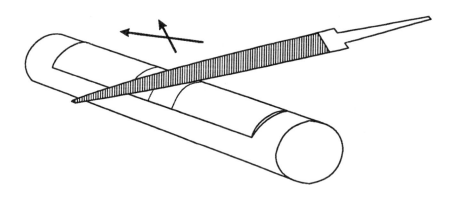

Figure 4.7. Modern bassoon shapers.

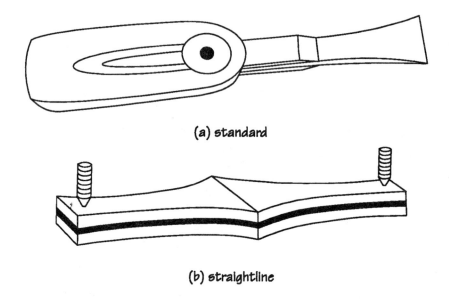

(a) standard

(b) straightline

reed making of earlier times[8]) and allows one to experiment with different shapes.

Small reeds can be made more quickly using a metal shaper. Such shapers can be fashioned from sheet brass (see Figure 4.8), such as that available from a hobby store. Cut the shaper to approximate size and then file it down to finished size.

Figure 4.8. Handmade shapers for shawm reeds.

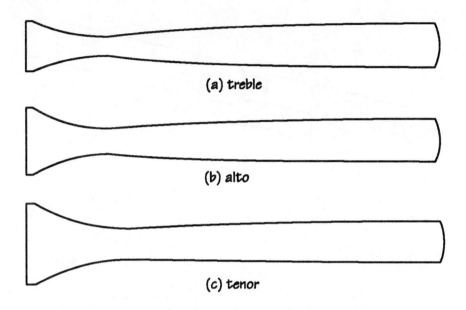

(a) treble

(b) alto

(c) tenor

When designing a shaper, keep in mind that the cane will shrink some after the reed has been constructed and allowed to dry. This shrinkage occurs primarily in the width of the reed, because of the characteristics of the cane fibers. Thus, if you are copying the shape of an old reed, make the new shape slightly oversized to ensure that the reed tube will be large enough to fit properly on the staple. If the shaper proves to be too large, it can easily be filed down. Also, allow about one millimeter extra at the tip for cutting open the reed, and make the shaper long enough so that it can be held comfortably. It can then be mounted in a wooden handle, or the end wrapped with tape, to make it more comfortable to hold.[9] The shaping of shawm reeds particularly is simplified by using a metal shaper be-cause their blades are fan-shaped.

After you have finished profiling, resoak the cane for a few moments if it has dried out. Make sure that you have made a clear score line at the center of the cane. Then, using the blade of the utility knife for support, fold the cane in half at the center, as shown in Figure 4.9. If you are shaping the reed by hand, draw the desired shape on the folded reed, as illustrated in Figure 4.10a. A template, such as that shown in Figure 4.10b, cut from stiff plastic or other suitable material may be used for this procedure, or it may be penciled in by sight.

Starting at the top (the widest part) of the shape, carefully trim the cane with

Figure 4.9. Folding the cane.

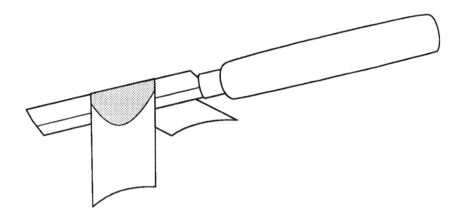

Figure 4.10. Shaping the cane.

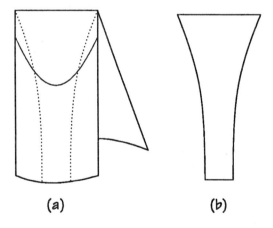

(a)   (b)

a very sharp cutting knife. Split off only a little of the cane at a time rather than trying to remove everything with one cut. This will minimize the danger of unwanted splitting. As you cut across the grain, take only a small amount and then allow the knife to follow the grain downward to split off that section of the cane. As you are performing this procedure, be careful not to squeeze the cane flat while holding it. This is the easiest way to crack the cane down the center and ruin it. Instead, focus on pushing downward on the knife blade while supporting the

Figure 4.11. Beveling the edges of the tube.

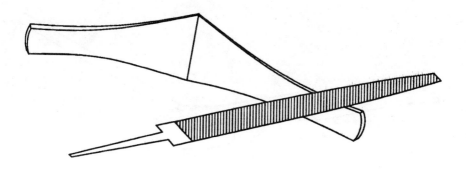

end of the cane rather than the sides. The cane will be quite fragile at this point, so proceed slowly and remove only small splinters of cane at a time. In addition, be sure that the knife is sharp at all times and that the cane has been properly soaked.

If you have made a metal shaper, the procedure is a bit simpler. After folding the cane, place it over the shaper blade. Grip the ends of the cane firmly with one hand to keep it in place, and with the utility knife trim the sides of the cane in a manner similar to that described above. As you remove splinters of cane, follow the metal shape with the knife blade until the shape of the cane matches that of the shaper blade. An X-*acto* knife is especially useful for shaping fan-shaped reeds because its thin blade can follow the shaper more easily. When shaping be careful not to push the shaper blade through the hinged part of the cane. This may happen if you are applying downward pressure on the cane while it is being held in place.

After the cane has been trimmed to size, finish the edges by sanding them with #320 wet-or-dry sandpaper until they are aligned exactly. If the butt ends of the reed are uneven, cut them to equal lengths. Finally, bevel the inside edges of the tube area with a knife or a file, as illustrated in Figure 4.11. This will improve the fit at the edges when the tube is formed around the mandrel and will help ensure an airtight fit around the staple.

Forming the Tube

Unfold the cane and place it on a cutting block or an easel. Using a single-edged razor blade or a sharp knife tip, score the ends of the cane lengthwise in the tube area (see Figure 4.12). The scores should run parallel about a millimeter or so

Figure 4.12. Scoring the cane.

apart. Cut lightly through the bark and then deepen the cut toward the butt of the reed. This scoring helps the cane to split evenly as it is formed around the mandrel. Since shawm reeds have such a short tube length, scoring the bark may be omitted.

Next, cut three lengths (about three inches) of #22 brass wire and place them on the reed, as shown in Figure 4.13. Shawm reeds require only two wires, and on treble shawm reeds you may wish to use #24 brass wire. Holding the wire horizontally and centered behind the tube area of the reed, bend the wire around the tube, crossing the ends of the wire on top. Continue bending the ends of the wire around until they are pointing away from you. The wire should circle the tube twice. Then form a twist with the ends so that the wire does not cross over itself except at the twist. (This procedure is much more difficult to describe than to do. The main objective is to get the wires to lie neatly in place.) The top wire is placed just below the blade area, and the bottom wire is placed at the butt of the reed. The middle wire is placed in between these two, closer to the top wire.

The practice of placing two wires, rather close together, in the middle of the reed is described in eighteenth- and early nineteenth-century tutors and is seen in surviving reeds.[10] The middle wire provides additional opportunities for making adjustments to blade tension. Its original purpose was probably to add strength to hold the throat of the reed open, since it was placed so close to the top wire.[11] Excessive rounding of these wires usually adds unwanted blade tension, which must be offset by further scraping. Changing the shape of the throat wires, for example, will produce variations in the equivalent volume and the reed resonance. Flattening the throat wires will usually make the low register more responsive because of the softening effect on the reed walls. However, the reed resonance will be lowered as well, and the blades may no longer be stiff enough

Figure 4.13. Placing the reed wires.

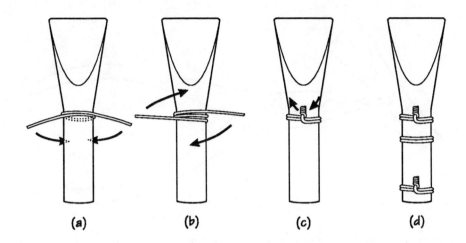

to facilitate the overblowing necessary to allow the upper-register notes to speak.

When using three wires, I recommend placing the upper two close together (e.g., five to seven millimeters apart for a bass curtal reed) in the manner of eighteenth-century bassoon reeds to minimize some of the complex situations that can occur when the center wire can be adjusted independently of the top wire. The top and middle wires should remain oval-shaped to allow the blades to follow the natural curvature of the cane. If the acoustic parameters of the reed need to be changed considerably, the top wire should be moved forward or back and the lay adjusted accordingly. The change is then accomplished by altering the blade length rather than by squeezing the throat wires, which primarily changes the lateral tension in the blades. Shawm reeds, of course, can have only two wires, since the tube of the reed is so short.

After the wires have been loosely placed in position, tighten the top wire. To do this, hold the tube firmly with one hand, grasp the twisted ends with a flat tip pliers, and pull straight away from the cane (see Figure 4.14). Finish this procedure by twisting up the slack. Brass wire will break easily if twisted while under tension, so it is important always to draw the wire tight by pulling straight from the tube and twist up the extra slack afterward. Be sure the top wire is tight, almost to the point of digging into the sides of the cane. This will prevent cracks from forming in the lay above the top wire when the tube is opened with the mandrel. The middle wire and the butt wire should be left slightly loose at this point.

To open the reed tube, gently squeeze the sides of the butt wire with a pliers

Figure 4.14. Tightening the wires.

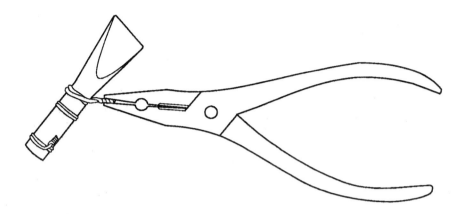

and carefully insert the mandrel between the two pieces of cane. Gradually work the reed onto the mandrel, kneading the tube with a needle-nosed pliers. If the mandrel cannot be worked into the tube easily, apply a small amount of beeswax to the end of the mandrel to reduce friction. Continue to open the tube until it has the desired diameter. This can be predetermined by placing your old reed on the mandrel to see how far down it fits.

After the tube has been rounded, tighten the bottom wire as described above. Remove the reed from the mandrel and check the butt for roundness. When you are satisfied with its looks, retighten both wires, clip off the excess wire (leaving five millimeters or so for later adjustments), and allow the reed to dry. If possible, dry the reed directly on the mandrel to help ensure that the tube forms a round opening. Scratch awls are inexpensive, so keep an extra one for this purpose. For some of the larger reed sizes, the pegs made for bassoon reed drying racks will work and can be purchased inexpensively from a double-reed supply house.

Another method for forming the reed tube, one advocated by many bassoon reed makers, is the hot mandrel system. This method is practical only for those reeds which have a long tube, thereby resembling bassoon reeds. For this method, fold the profiled cane in half and wrap the tube end with a flat shoestring or a piece of heavy string, ending with a half-hitch in the blade area (see Figure 4.15). Soak the wrapped cane for several minutes. Next, heat the mandrel over a flame for about a minute, but not longer lest the cane become singed when the tube is opened. Using the jaws of a pliers, gently squeeze the butt end of the cane open and insert the hot mandrel. After putting down the pliers, grasp the reed at its throat and push it straight onto the mandrel without twisting until the correct

Figure 4.15. Wrapping the reed with heavy string.

size opening has been achieved. Unwrap the upper part of the string down to the region of the top wire. Affix the top wire and tighten, as described above. Finally, after removing the rest of the string, position and tighten the middle and butt wires, and allow the reed to dry.

Binding

The reed should be allowed to dry for at least 24 hours before the binding is applied. The cane will have shrunk some after drying, so retighten the wires and cut off the wire twists to about four or five millimeters in length. Coat the tube between the bottom two wires with a waterproof glue such as *Duco Cement*, and wrap the area between the wires with nylon string. Finish by fastening the string securely with a half-hitch and coating the entire string surface generously with *Duco Cement*. Place the reed on a drying rack (or leave it on the mandrel), and allow the glue to dry for several hours or overnight. After the glue has dried, bend the wire ends down against the tube.

This type of binding will not separate from the cane and will allow the entire reed to be immersed in water when the blades are being wetted for use. The binding process can also be done after finishing the lay of the reed. Many makers form a ball of string over the butt wire in the style of modern bassoon reeds. It has a pleasant appearance but is not necessary for strengthening the binding. Shawm reeds should not be wrapped with a ball of string around the butt wire in this fashion unless there is enough clearance for it in the pirouette.

Figure 4.16. Cutting open the tip.

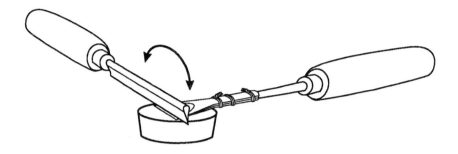

Scraping

The reed is now ready for working on the scrape. Soak the blades of the reed (but not the tube) in water for about fifteen minutes. Next, place the reed on the mandrel and cut open the tip, as illustrated in Figure 4.16. This is done with a utility knife or single-edged razor blade and the cutting block. Place the tip of the reed on the block. Then place the knife blade on the cane about a millimeter from the reed tip and bear down, using a rocking motion to cut through the cane. Do not use a sawing motion for this procedure, and take care not to let the knife skid as you bear down on the cane with the blade. (A sharp scissors also provides a quick and effective method for opening the tip.) The corners should also be trimmed (see Figure 4.17) to help prevent splits along the sides of the reed if it is accidentally bumped at the corners.[12]

Next, place the reed on its staple or bocal. If it does not fit far enough onto the staple, enlarge the reed tube with a reamer or a round needle file. This procedure should be done while the cane is dry to avoid tearing the fibers. Then, with the reed on the staple, place a finger over the lower end of the staple, and blow through the reed to check for leakage. If a bubbling or hissing sound is heard, there probably is a leak where the reed tube fits the staple or at the edges of the blades. If the blades are leaking, adjust the top wire as shown in Figure 4.18, or sand the edges. If the reed tube appears to be leaking, first check that the staple is round. Then ream or file the reed tube until the leak is fixed. Another solution for a leaky reed is to heat the mandrel, press it into some beeswax, and then use it to coat the inside of the reed tube. This should also be done when the reed is dry so that the wax can penetrate and adhere to the cane fibers.

To finish the lay, place the reed on the mandrel and insert a plaque into the tip between the blades. (Avoid contoured plaques except when scraping larger

Figure 4.17. Clipping the corners of the tip.

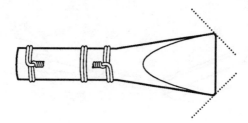

Figure 4.18. Adjusting the tip opening of the reed.

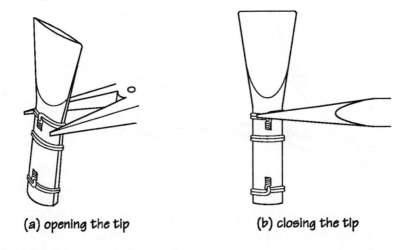

(a) opening the tip   **(b) closing the tip**

reeds.) Plastic guitar picks are ideal, as they will not damage the edge of the knife, as a metal plaque can during the scraping process. A scraping knife is used to remove cane when finishing the lay. During the scraping process, rest the knife blade against the thumb, perpendicular to the cane. Then use a rocking motion to remove wood, as illustrated in Figure 4.19. The knife blade must be kept very sharp at all times so that a minimum of downward pressure need be applied. Always scrape towards the tip of the reed.

If the knife does not cut easily, it should be sharpened before proceeding further. Scraping with a dull knife usually leads to increased downward pressure on the cane in an effort to force the knife blade to dig into the cane. This will compress the cane fibers rather than cut through them, and the blade may also split

Figure 4.19. Scraping the blades.

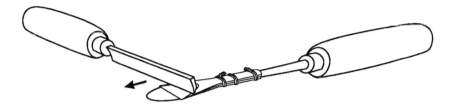

Figure 4.20. Filing the tip.

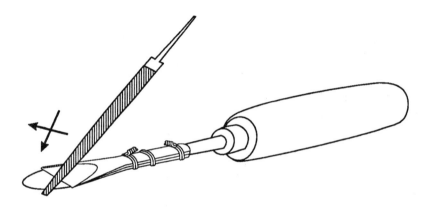

from the downward pressure being applied to the natural arch of the cane. (Directions for sharpening knives are found at the end of Chapter 3.)

Files may also be used in finishing the lay (see Figure 4.20) and are especially useful for smoothing out any bumps left by scraping. The reed tip can be thinned with the scraping knife (Figure 4.21) or with wet-or-dry sandpaper. To sand the tip of small reeds, place the reed on the mandrel but do not insert the plaque. While holding some #320 wet-or-dry sandpaper in place on a flat surface, carefully sand the corners and the tip of the reed by sliding the reed blade back and forth across the sandpaper surface, stabilizing the top side of the blade area with your index finger (see Figure 4.22). Proceed slowly and check your work often when using this method, as it is easy to sand through the blade very quickly.

When an acceptable scrape has been achieved, the finished lay can be polished with #600 wet-or-dry sandpaper or Dutch rush. During the first several days the reed may change as it settles into its new shape. The cane fibers tend to expand (or "grow"), so the reed may require more scraping. These changes can be min-

Figure 4.21. Thinning the tip with a knife.

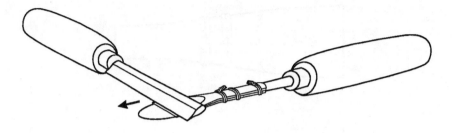

Figure 4.22. Sanding the tip.

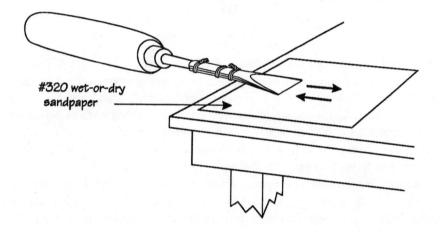

#320 wet-or-dry
sandpaper

imized if the cane is prepared before reed construction begins with the alternate soaking and drying cycles as described earlier in this chapter.

Although we know virtually nothing about how double reeds were scraped during the Renaissance, we do have much indirect information to draw from when choosing an appropriate scrape for a particular instrument. We have already considered our most important resource here, the acoustic requirements of surviving instruments. In addition, we can examine the styles of scrape used in eighteenth-century bassoon reed making as well as in modern reed making in order to get a clearer idea of the possibilities available to us.

The composition of *Arundo donax* can be divided into several layers of differing density.[13] The densest area is the thin layer of bark on the outside. Below this lies

Figure 4.23. Eighteenth-century bassoon reed scrapes.

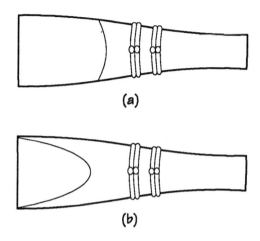

a thin layer of softer but tough fibers. Farther inside the cane tube is the *paren-chyme*, a much softer material characterized by its grainy appearance. This layer becomes progressively softer and spongier as one moves toward the center of the cane tube. The relative density of the finished blade is determined by what part of the cane tube it is fashioned from. Thus, gouging more thinly will bring the blades into the denser area of the *parenchyme*, while using a thicker gouge favors the spongier layers farther inside the tube.

Modern bassoon reeds are usually scraped in one of two styles. The German-style scrape has a center spine that travels the length of the reed (see Figure 1.14b). All the bark is removed from the blade area. The spine of this type of reed is made of the denser fibers below the bark, while the sides are scraped quite thin, down to the spongier area of the *parenchyme*. The French scrape, on the other hand, is scraped with a more even taper from the top wire to the tip (see Figure 1.14a).[14] Only the tip of this reed contains the softest portion of the cane tube, and the blades are left thicker along the edges. The tip of the German scrape tends to close last in the center because of the prominent center spine, and this results in a darker tone quality. In the French scrape the tip closes more evenly across, and this encourages a brighter sonority.

Judging from surviving eighteenth-century reeds and from the scraping rec-ommendations found in historical bassoon tutors, two types of scrape seem to have been used at that time, and both are similar to the modern French scrape.[15] The first type employs an even taper from the tip to the throat area, sometimes with some of the bark left on the back of the blade, as illustrated in Figure 4.23a. The second type resembles the scrape of the eighteenth-century oboe reed. A wedge-shaped center cut has been taken so that the softest area of cane is in the center of the tip, and thicker spine-like areas follow the edges of the blade down to the tip (see Figure 4.23b). Bark is often left on the blade area, giving a V-shaped appearance. This type of reed was usually thinned on the underside of the blades during gouging in order to leave dense cane material down the edges of the blades. These two styles of scrape are both very similar to the modern French scrape in that both have a uniformly thinned tip with denser areas along the edges of the blades.

Before choosing a style of scrape for a particular instrument, we must review the acoustic requirements of the scrape. First of all, the blades need to be of an appropriate length and possess enough longitudinal stiffness to provide the correct parameters for the reed resonance and to facilitate overblowing. Although the total equivalent volume of a reed need not be affected by varying the shape, the length of the blades do affect the reed resonance by determining its upper limit. Thus, a longitudinal spine or stiffness of some sort is advantageous for the proper placement of the reed resonance, for minimizing unwanted embouchure manipulation of the reed resonance, and for allowing notes to be overblown with ease.

Second, the transverse stiffness must be rigid enough to maintain a proper tip opening. The amount of stiffness across the blades interacts with the embouchure's ability to manipulate the size of the tip opening. This stiffness is affected by the natural curvature of the cane, artificial tension from wires, and the density and thickness of cane in the lay.

Third, the tip must close in a proper manner for the best tone production and a desirable timbre. A tip that closes last in the center will generate less energy into the upper partials of the tone, while a tip that snaps shut will generate more. The latter produces a brighter timbre and adds to the stability of the instrument, while a tip that closes asymmetrically is less predictable and therefore undesirable. The particular type of tip closure is determined by the transverse flexibility and evenness of the blades.

In reviewing these points, it becomes more obvious that the modern German bassoon scrape is not the most desirable choice for many early woodwinds. The modern French scrape (or some variation of it) is really more suited to the demands placed on the reeds of Renaissance woodwinds. German-style reeds are more successful on larger instruments than on smaller ones. If you do choose to make reeds with a center spine, avoid rounding the throat wires, and scrape the tip area so that it snaps shut in one motion. This will allow a larger proportion of upper partials to be generated for added tonal stability.

V

SHAWM REEDS

The majority of reeds, staples, and pirouettes of historical shawms in museums have unfortunately long been lost.[1] The reconstruction of these critical components of the instrument must therefore be accomplished through the indirect information we have at our disposal. This includes the study of the acoustic requirements of the instrument, iconographic evidence of reed and pirouette set-ups, depictions of embouchure, and an examination of modern descendants of the shawm.

The acoustic design of the "classic" western European shawms, as depicted by Praetorius (see Figure 5.1) and exemplified by museum specimens, has already been discussed in Chapter 1. Iconography suggests that the designs for the treble and alto sizes were already established by the beginning of the fifteenth century.[2] The lengthening of the bell section on the treble shawm by this time improved stability and added subtlety to playing techniques. This technological achievement is also just one indication that lip control was being used in shawm technique by the early fifteenth century. The fact that the shawm had no thumb hole and possessed a range of about an octave and a fifth suggests that a rather sophisticated method of playing was employed.[3] Shawmists are most often depicted with puffed cheeks in iconography, an embouchure style that would afford a loud, bright sound for outdoor playing, yet still allow necessary lip control over the reed.

Detailed information about the shape of the reed and pirouette can also be gleaned from several sources. Mersenne provides a clear (if somewhat crude) woodcut of an alto shawm, pirouette, and reed (see Figure 5.2).[4] The reed is fan-shaped, and the staple appears to extend to the top of the pirouette. In addition, the shawms depicted in Renaissance and early Baroque paintings show a similar style of reed and pirouette combination.[5]

Dimensions for treble and alto shawms with their reeds, pirouettes, and staples were recorded in a late seventeenth-century manuscript by James Talbot. These measurements are given in Figure 5.4.[6] While the date of this manuscript is rather

Figure 5.1. Renaissance shawms. Praetorius, *De Organographia*, 1619.

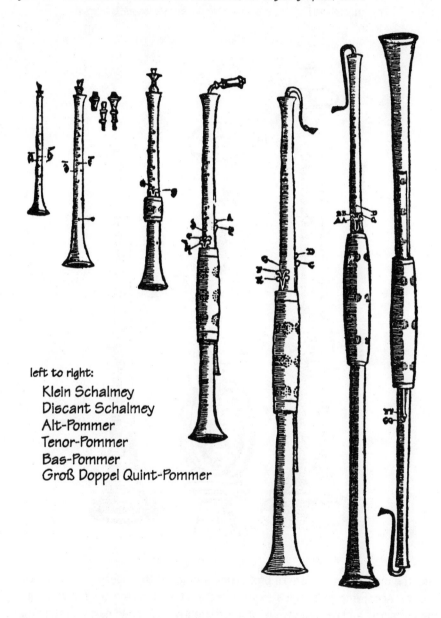

left to right:
   Klein Schalmey
   Discant Schalmey
   Alt-Pommer
   Tenor-Pommer
   Bas-Pommer
   Groß Doppel Quint-Pommer

Figure 5.2. Alto and treble shawms, showing details of the keywork and
pirouette of the alto shawm. Mersenne, *Harmonie Universelle*,
1636.

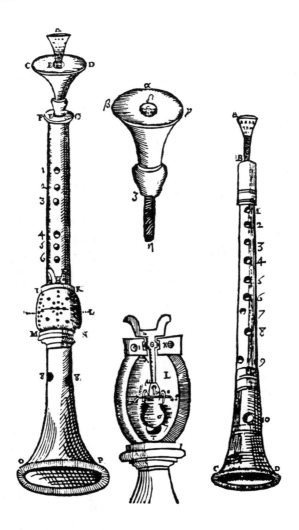

late, the measurements are of proportion similar to the older Praetorius style of
shawm. According to Talbot's measurements, the staples extend slightly above
the pirouette, and the reeds appear to be slightly longer and narrower than those
depicted in Renaissance artwork. More important, they clearly indicate the proportions of cane length to staple length, a critical factor in determining the proper
placement of the reed resonance.

Figure 5.3. Shawms. Mersenne, *Harmonie Universelle*, 1636.

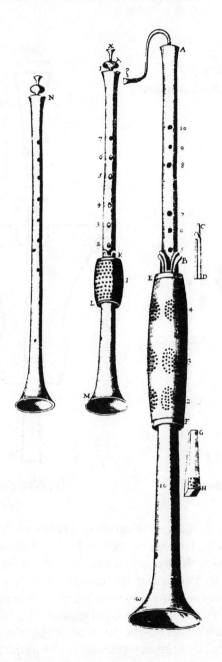

Figure 5.4. Shawm reed and pirouette measurements from James Talbot's manuscript (c. 1695).

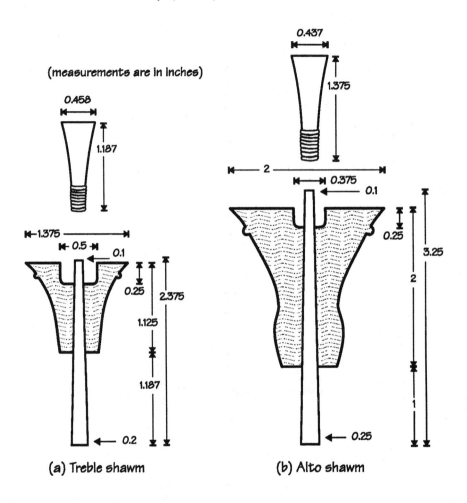

(a) Treble shawm   (b) Alto shawm

The modern Catalan shawms, as depicted in Figure 5.5, have a similarly styled pirouette with a short, fan-shaped reed and a long bell section similar to the shawms of earlier periods. The reed designs of the Catalan shawms have been described by Anthony Baines and are reproduced in Figure 5.6.[7] These instruments (*tiple* and *tenora*) are direct descendants of the Renaissance treble shawm and have been fitted with nonstandardized keywork.

Shawms which do not have the characteristic bell section of the classic Renaissance shawm may be classified as folk shawms, such as the Spanish *dulzaina* (see

Figure 5.5. Twentieth-century Catalan shawms.

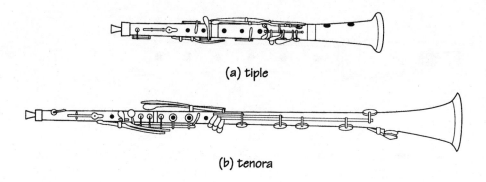

(a) tiple

(b) tenora

Figure 5.6. Twentieth-century Catalan shawms. Detail by Anthony Baines of the reed and pirouette of the *tenora* and *tiple*.

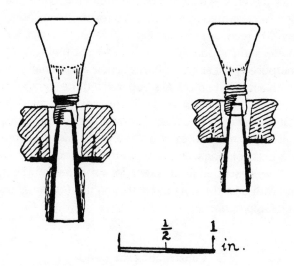

Figure 5.7). The *dulzaina* is a keyless, modern Spanish shawm with a short bell section and is similar to a bagpipe chanter. It is played without a pirouette. Shawm-like instruments without the characteristic long, resonating bell sections have existed in many cultures as folk instruments. This distinction is an important one, for it was not until the development of the oboe in the seventeenth century that the two separate and distinct types of instruments were merged into one.[8]

Figure 5.7. Twentieth-century Spanish *dulzaina*.

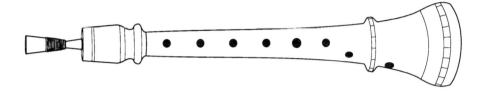

The differences in the bore design and the pirouette assembly among the various makes of reproduction shawms pose a major problem in designing reeds for them. It is interesting that while the Renaissance shawm has had a consistently recognizable and characteristic design from the early fifteenth century on, to date very few modern builders have been able to reconstruct a shawm that is based on historical evidence. Rather than using a historical (and acoustically appropriate) reed setup, such as can still be found on the twentieth-century Catalan shawms, modern builders have commonly employed a pirouette with a deep cavity to admit a long, bassoon-like reed, as shown in Figure 5.8a. By placing the reed resonance very low, this latter setup produces an uncharacteristic timbre and tends to negate the acoustic purpose of the elongated bell section. Additionally, retrofitting these instruments with a more appropriate setup may require some extensive retuning to enable the bell section to stabilize the instrument properly. Also, unwanted co-operations that did not exist when a longer, oversized reed was employed may occur among the upper resonances. Therefore, when making a reed for such an instrument, the best solution may be to copy the old reed or to make a small, bassoon-style reed, as described in Chapter 6 for curtal reeds.[9] The instrument can then be played with or without its pirouette and used in situations where a folk shawm might be appropriate.

Constructing the Reed

The following reed-making instructions are intended for shawms which have been designed to use a short, fan-shaped style of reed in a pirouette and which are meant to be played with a loose, but controlled, embouchure. The exact dimensions given here are suggested as points of departure and may need to be adjusted according the particular instrument being fitted and one's embouchure preferences. Initially, one should copy an old reed (preferably one that still works)

Figure 5.8. Modern shawm pirouettes and their reed designs.

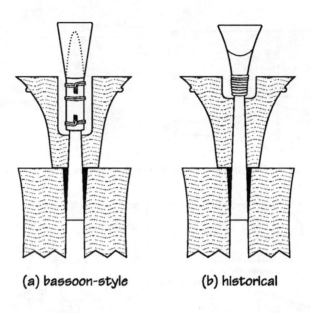

(a) bassoon-style   (b) historical

and then make adjustments and improvements until the new reed produces de-sired characteristics. Specific reed-making instructions common to all types of reeds (gouging, profiling, shaping, and binding) are found in Chapter 4. Bass shawm reeds (as well as reeds for other shawms which may require a bassoon-like shape to fit a pirouette, as shown in Figure 5.8a) are similar in design to cur-tal reeds. These are discussed in Chapter 6.

Treble, alto, and tenor shawm reeds are all similarly constructed and can be made from either bassoon cane tubes, gouged cane, or extra-wide profiled cane. (Regular shaped and profiled bassoon cane is too narrow and is usually profiled too thin for use here.) If you are using a bassoon tube, first split the tube into sections. Then gouge the cane to a thickness of about 1 mm (.040″) in the center, becoming slightly thinner at the sides. Cut the gouged cane to the proper length according to the given dimensions, mark the center, and profile, as shown by the shaded areas in Figure 5.9.

If you are starting with gouged cane, either gouged bassoon or contrabassoon cane can be used. If you have tools for hand gouging, thin the gouge to about 1 mm (.040″) in the center and slightly thinner on the sides. If you do not have goug-ing tools, sand the inside of the cane with wet-or-dry sandpaper wrapped around a dowel to reduce the gouge thickness. Cut the gouged cane to the proper length

Figure 5.9 Shawm reed measurements.

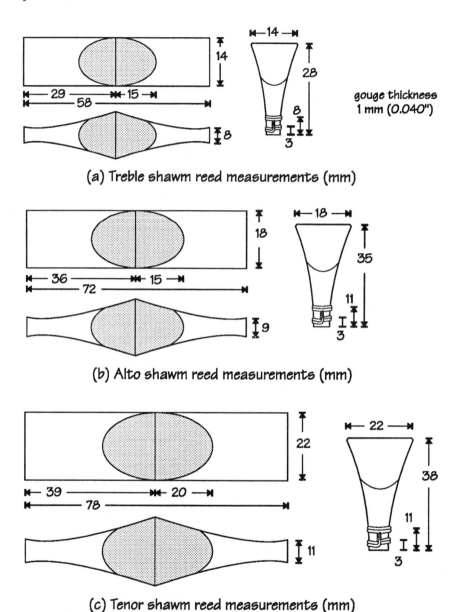

gouge thickness
1 mm (0.040")

(a) Treble shawm reed measurements (mm)

(b) Alto shawm reed measurements (mm)

(c) Tenor shawm reed measurements (mm)

Figure 5.10. Shaping the cane.

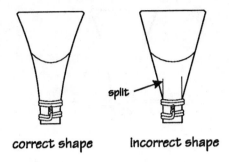

correct shape   incorrect shape

according to given dimensions, mark the center, and profile, as shown by the shaded areas in Figure 5.9. The amount of wood removed during profiling will, of course, depend on the gouge thickness.

If you are using extra-wide profiled cane, sand the inside of the cane lightly to smooth it, and cut the ends of the cane to proper length. Although the gouge thickness cannot be altered, the chief advantage for the use of this type of cane lies in the fact that it saves a great deal of time by eliminating the steps of gouging and profiling by hand. I also recommend that beginners use this type of cane in order to obtain a finished product as quickly and effortlessly as possible. Hand gouging and hand profiling are techniques that can be learned and then added to one's reed-making skills at a later time.

After the cane has been profiled, fold it in half and shape it. The shape should flare somewhat so that the expansion begins above the top wire. This will prevent the sides from splitting along the grain near the wire (see Figure 5.10). The exact width of the shape at the base will depend upon the diameter of the staple at the point where the butt of the reed fits. To determine this width, multiply the diameter of the staple at this point by 3.14 and divide by two. Another method is to wrap a piece of string or wire around the staple at the point where the butt of the reed will fit. Measure this length and divide by two. For either method allow a bit extra for shrinkage when the cane dries.

The base of the reed shape should have a slight flare, as shown in Figure 5.9. This will ensure a proper, tapered fit around the conical staple, and it will help maintain a proper tip opening. The cane can be hand-shaped by using the utility knife, or a metal shaper fashioned from sheet brass (as described in Chapter 4) can be used.

After sanding the edges of the shaped cane, unfold it, and bevel the lower inside

Figure 5.11. Placing the wires.

edges of the tube. Next, score the bark (if necessary), refold the cane, and place two wires at the base, as shown in Figure 5.11. Draw the top wire tight to prevent cracks from forming down the center of the blade when the mandrel is inserted.

Carefully work the mandrel into the end of the reed tube to the proper depth, then tighten the bottom wire. This step should be done with care so that the reed will form a tight seal with the staple. Cut off the excess wire. Finally, sand the sides of the reed until they are uniform and flush. Cut off the tip, and, if necessary, squeeze the top wire to open or close the blades as needed.

If enough wood was removed during the profiling process, the reed should now produce a sound. At this point it is a good idea to place the reed onto its staple to check the fit. If the reed pushes too far onto the staple, the shape at the butt may have been too wide. If further tightening of the bottom wire does not sufficiently reduce the size of the tube, remove the wires and reshape the butt. Then reassemble the reed and check for a proper fit on the staple. If the tube is too narrow to fit far enough onto the staple, it can be reamed out after it dries.

Allow the reed to dry completely, for at least 24 hours. The cane will shrink some during drying, so place the reed on the mandrel and retighten the wires. Trim the excess wire to about three or four millimeters, but do not bend the wire ends down yet. Coat the area below the top wire with *Duco Cement*, and wrap the area between the wires with some nylon string, tying it off with a half-hitch. A ball of string can be wrapped over the bottom wire, but be sure to allow enough room for the reed to fit into the pirouette. Apply a coat of *Duco Cement* over the string, and allow it to dry. Trim the bottom wire close to the base, leaving one or two twists to hold it in place, and bend the tips of the top wire down flat.

Next, wet the blades of the reed and place it on the staple. For treble and alto reeds, the top wire should be level with the top of the pirouette. Also, the top wire must be above the tip of the staple so that it can be adjusted without flattening the staple. If the reed does not fit far enough onto the staple, enlarge the tube of the reed with a needle file. Finally, block the end of the staple with your finger and blow through the reed to check for leakage around the butt of the reed. If there is any leakage, check to see that the bottom wire is round, and file the inside of the tube with a needle file until a proper fit is achieved. The reed is now ready for final scraping.

Scraping the Reed

The scrape should satisfy three basic conditions: (1) the reed should be free-blowing and tongue easily in all registers; (2) the reed should function well acoustically to provide optimum performance and proper tuning; and (3) the reed should provide a desirable tone color. The easiest and most useful scrape for treble, alto, and tenor shawm reeds is a straight taper from the beginning of the lay to the tip of the blade, as shown in Figure 5.12a.

Figure 5.12. Scraping the lay of the shawm reed.

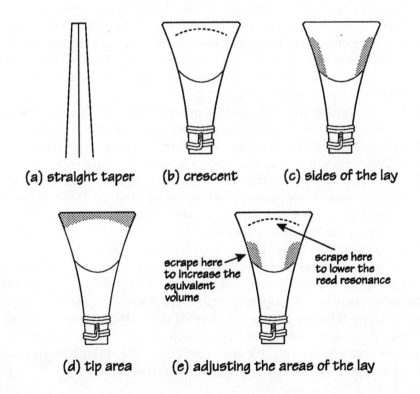

(a) straight taper   (b) crescent   (c) sides of the lay

(d) tip area   (e) adjusting the areas of the lay

scrape here
to increase the
equivalent
volume

scrape here
to lower the
reed resonance

Figure 5.13. Shawm reed tip openings.

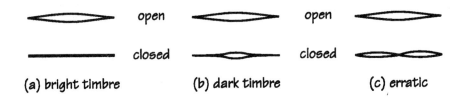

(a) bright timbre   (b) dark timbre   (c) erratic

Begin by removing wood, using knife strokes diagonally from the center of the blade. Some cane may also need to be removed along the sides and tip. When viewed from the side, the blades should be left as thick as possible and should gradually taper toward the tip. The fanned part of the blades should be thinner toward the edges and should show a crescent-shaped pattern when held up to a strong light. This is represented by the dotted line in Figure 5.12b.

Next, check the closing of the reed tip. To do this, place your thumb and first finger on the reed at the point where your embouchure would normally be positioned, and squeeze the blades gently. (Be sure the reed has been soaked properly before performing this procedure.) The blades should touch at all points simultaneously (Figure 5.13a) or close last at the very center (Figure 5.13b). A reed which closes in one motion (as in Figure 5.13a) will produce the brightest timbre, while a reed which never completely closes at the center (Figure 5.13b) will produce the darkest tone. Thus, a darker tone quality may be attained by leaving more wood in the center of the tip than at the sides.

If the reed closes in the center first (as in Figure 5.13c), an unstable acoustic situation will occur during playing: a portion of the air blown into the instrument will not cooperate with the oscillation of the reed to stabilize a note. This type of tip closure usually results from the edges of the blade tip being stiffer than the center. If the corners seem too thick, sand them and recheck the tip closure. If this does not help, remove more wood along the sides of the lay (as shown in Figure 5.12c), or trim a bit from the tip, and then rebalance the tip opening.

Some common tip irregularities are depicted in Figure 5.14. These are due primarily to an unevenly scraped tip area and should be avoided.

When the tip has been determined to have a desirable closure, place the reed on its pirouette-plus-staple setup and sound the pitch obtained by using the same embouchure as when playing the instrument. The pitch produced should be near the octave of the low-register note fingered 123 ————. This pitch is approximately A_5 for a treble shawm in D, D_5 for an alto shawm in G, and G_4 for a tenor shawm in C (see Figure 5.15). The exact reed-plus-staple driving frequency can also be determined by using an old reed which is known to work well.

Figure 5.14. Irregular tip openings.

(a) (b) (c) (d)

Figure 5.15. Approximate reed-plus-staple driving frequencies for shawms.

Treble in D   Alto in G   Tenor in C   Bass in F

This simple diagnostic test will tell you whether the reed meets its acoustic requirements for playing the lower register in tune. If this pitch is unstable, the tip may be too open or the blades may be too thin. If the pitch is too high, the tip may be too closed, or the lay may need to be lengthened or thinned. On the other hand, if the note is too low, the tip may be too open, or the lay may need to be shortened by trimming the tip. When the proper reed-plus-staple driving frequency can be sounded, place the setup on the instrument and play the lower octave of the instrument.

If the reed tongues poorly in the low register, thin the tip area (the shaded area in Figure 5.12d). Proceed slowly, because if the area just behind the tip becomes too thin, the reed will not respond well in the upper register. When making these adjustments, the tip opening may also change and need to be adjusted by squeezing the top wire.

Next, check the pitch of the note fingered 123 4567 by comparing it with a tuning standard. If this note is sharp, continue to thin the blades toward the back of the lay, as shown in Figure 5.12e. Then check this note with its octave. If the upper note is sharp in relation to its lower octave, the equivalent volume of the reed is too small. Continue to scrape the back of the lay until the notes of the lower register are properly tuned.

If the blades become too soft during this process, however, all pitches will become unstable, and the reed will be very difficult to overblow. If this occurs, it may be necessary to redesign the reed with a slightly longer blade length.

Now check the tuning of the first five notes of the instrument with their octaves

Figure 5.16. Tuning the octaves of the lower register.

(see Figure 5.16). This test helps to determine whether the reed resonance has been correctly located. If the octaves overblow flat, the reed resonance needs to be raised by shortening the blade length of the reed or by closing the tip opening slightly. Conversely, if the octaves overblow sharp, the tip opening should be increased, or the lay of the reed should be thinned at the area just behind the tip (see Figure 5.12e). This is a critical area for the ability of the reed to overblow properly, so exercise caution when scraping this region. As previously stated, excessive thinning will lead to a flabby, unstable reed. Also, a tip opening that is too large may lead to an unstable situation, while a tip that is too closed will hamper the production of low notes and restrict the ability of the embouchure to make the fine adjustments to the reed resonance that are necessary for good tuning. A balance must therefore be struck between the stiffness of the blades and the size of the tip opening.

If, after adjusting the reed resonance, the equivalent volume has become mismatched to the instrument, the staple length should be adjusted until the lower register is again properly aligned. This procedure will probably not be necessary, as the initial adjustments to the equivalent volume should also bring the reed resonance into alignment for good response in the upper register.

Finally, test the tuning of the different registers by comparing the lowest note of the instrument with its second and third octaves (i.e., D_5 and D_6 for a treble shawm in D), as shown in Figure 5.17. Checking the tuning of the third-octave note requires knowing your instrument well enough to be able to play this note with a harmonic fingering. Good harmonic alignment in this area will ensure maximum stability in the usable range of the instrument and can be helpful for diagnosing a problem in the reed. Since the note in the third octave lies near the reed resonance, it is quite sensitive to the exact placement of the reed resonance, while the second-octave note is more dependent upon the total equivalent volume of the reed cavity and staple for its proper tuning.[10] If the third-octave note cannot be coaxed from the instrument, the reed may be too large to allow the production of harmonics in this area. If the note is flat, the reed blades may need to be shortened. If the note is sharp, the lay should be lengthened or scraped, or both.

Figure 5.17. Tuning the upper register.

Treble shawm   Alto shawm   Tenor shawm

If the reed does not respond well in the upper register, thin the tip area (the shaded area in Figure 5.12d), being careful not to disturb the area of the lay just behind the tip.

On a well-designed instrument, the appropriate equivalent volume for low notes and reed resonance for proper tuning of higher partials will be related so that making adjustments to correct one parameter will also correct the other. Additionally, this relationship between the equivalent volume and the reed resonance allows one to make small changes to either parameter by embouchure adjustment for tuning purposes without resorting to extremely different embouchures for the different registers of the instrument. Thus, once you have adjusted the reed for playing the fundamental register in tune, you will most likely also have brought the reed resonance into position for good cooperation of upper resonances.

VI

CURTAL REEDS

Curtal reeds are perhaps more similar to bassoon reeds than any of the other styles used on Renaissance woodwinds. The earliest known written sources on reed making date from the second half of the eighteenth century and the early nineteenth century.[1] Among the earliest tutors with detailed instructions for bassoon reed making is Etienne Ozi's *Méthode nouvelle et raisonnee pour le basson* (Paris, 1787).[2] While Ozi's tutor was published a hundred years after the curtal fell into disuse and is admittedly quite late for our purposes, the many similarities in bore design and playing technique between the two instruments warrant a closer look at Ozi's reed design and scraping methods. Ozi's reed and its measurements are reproduced in Figures 6.1 and 6.2.

According to Ozi, the cane should be gouged to half a *ligne* (1.1 mm, or .043")[3] and scraped more at the center, where the cane is folded. A single band of iron wire was formed with an oval-shaped mandrel and placed at the center of the reed.[4] Ozi's illustration of the reed depicts a V-shaped scrape beginning midway between the tip and the top wire, and his description of the scraping method implies that a wedge-like cut is to be made from a point five *lignes* (11.3 mm) above the top wire to the tip area. This type of scrape has much in common with the modern French scrape.

Most of the surviving bassoon reeds from the late eighteenth century have been constructed in a manner similar to Ozi's reed.[5] While the gouge thickness seems to have been somewhat thinner than that used for modern bassoon reeds, it must also be remembered that additional thinning of the gouge at the center region is equivalent to making the blade portion of the reed from a very thinly gouged piece of cane. This type of reed combines the stiffness of a hard reed (by using the stiffer cane near the bark) with the responsiveness of a softer reed (since the blades are quite thin) and is therefore well suited to our purposes.

The curtals and bassoons illustrated by Mersenne and Praetorius in the early seventeenth century have been reproduced in Figures 6.3 and 6.4. Mersenne's il-

Figure 6.1. Ozi's bassoon reed (1803).

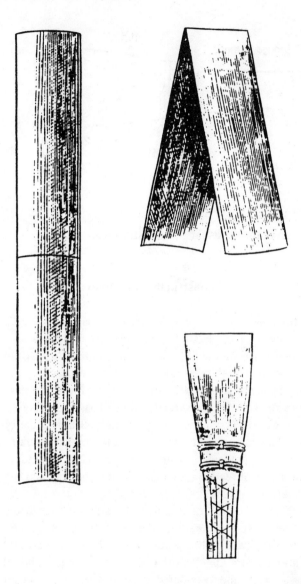

Figure 6.2. Ozi's bassoon reed measurements (1803).

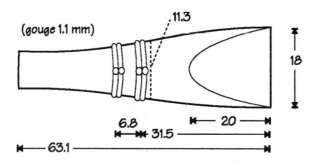

lustrations are rather crude, and neither source offers much detailed information about the design of the reeds for these instruments.

Constructing the Reed

Approximate dimensions for alto, tenor, and bass curtal reeds and a bass shawm reed have been provided in Figures 6.5 and 6.6 as suggested points of departure. Because of the variety of designs found among the instruments of modern builders and personal preferences in embouchure formation, the exact dimensions of these reeds may need to be modified to suit a particular instrument. In particular, the tube of the reed may need to be lengthened or shortened according to the way the bocal has been proportioned. If possible, one should initially copy the dimensions of an old reed and then make adjustments and improvements until it produces desired characteristics. Detailed instructions common to all types of reeds (gouging, profiling, shaping, and binding) can be found in Chapter 4.

The different sizes of curtal reeds are all similarly constructed and can be fashioned from either bassoon cane tubes, gouged cane, or extra-wide profiled cane. If you are using tube cane, split the tube into sections and gouge the cane to a thickness of about 1 mm (.040″) in the center, becoming slightly thinner at the sides. Cut the gouged cane to the proper length according to given dimensions, mark the center, and profile.

If you are starting with gouged cane, either bassoon or contrabassoon cane can be used. If you have tools for hand gouging, thin the gouge to about 1 mm (.040″) in the center and slightly thinner on the sides. If you do not have a gouging tool,

Figure 6.3. Curtals and bassoons. Mersenne, *Harmonie Universelle*,
1636.

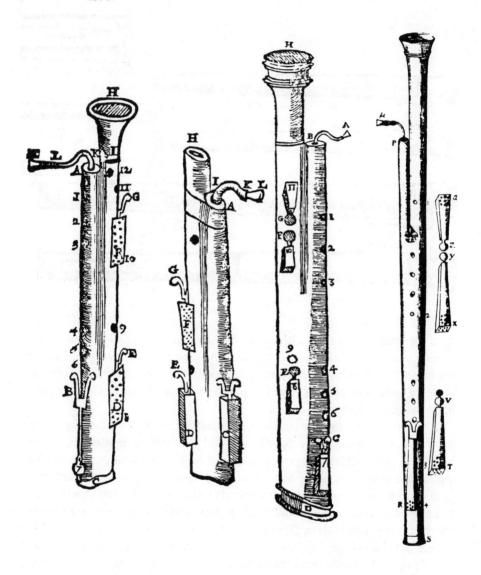

Figure 6.4. Curtals. Praetorius, *De Organographia*, 1619.

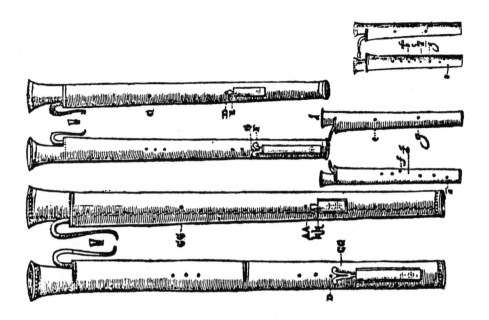

sand the inside of the cane with wet-or-dry sandpaper wrapped around a dowel to reduce the gouge thickness. Cut the gouged cane to the proper length according to given dimensions, mark the center, and profile. The amount of wood that needs to be removed during profiling and the exact length of the lay will depend upon the gouge thickness.

If you are using extra-wide profiled cane, sand the inside of the cane lightly and cut the ends of the cane to proper length. Although the gouge thickness cannot be altered, the chief advantage of this type of cane is that it saves time by eliminating the steps of gouging and profiling by hand. Beginners will also benefit from using it, as they will obtain a finished product as quickly and effortlessly as possible. Hand gouging and profiling are techniques that can be learned and then added to one's reed-making skills at a later time.

Next, fold and shape the cane. The exact width of the shape at the base will depend upon the diameter of the bocal at the point where the butt of the reed fits. To determine this width, multiply the diameter by 3.14 and divide by two. Another method is to wrap a piece of string or wire around the bocal at the point where the butt of the reed will fit. Measure this length and divide by two. For either method allow a bit extra for shrinkage when the cane dries. The tube area of

Figure 6.5. Curtal reed measurements.

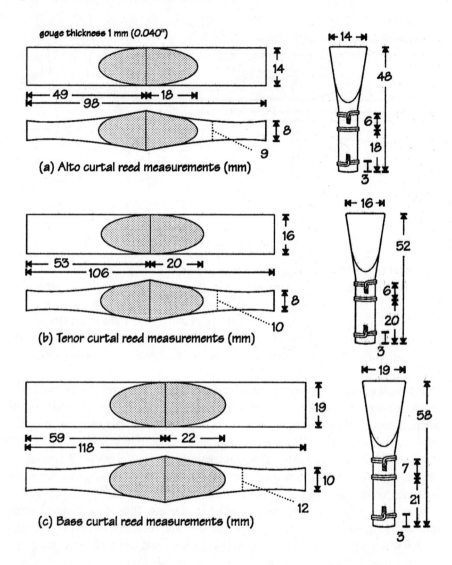

(a) Alto curtal reed measurements (mm)

(b) Tenor curtal reed measurements (mm)

(c) Bass curtal reed measurements (mm)

the shape should have a slight waist, so that the ends of the cane appear to flare slightly.

After sanding the edges of the shaped cane, unfold it, and bevel the lower inside edges of the tube. Next, score the bark, refold the cane, and place three wires as shown in Figure 6.7. (If you are using two wires instead of three, omit the middle

Figure 6.6. Bass shawm reed measurements.

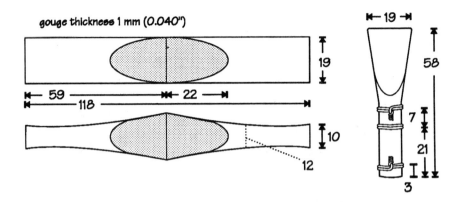

one.) Draw the top wire tight in order to help prevent cracks from forming down the center of the blades when the tube is formed.

Gently squeeze open the butt wire, work the mandrel into the end of the reed tube until it has been inserted to the proper depth, and tighten the wires. This step should be done with care so that the reed will form a tight seal with the bocal. Trim off the excess wire and sand the sides of the reed until they are flush. Next, cut off the tip and, if necessary, squeeze the top wire to open or close the blades as needed.

If enough wood was removed during the profiling process, the reed should now produce a sound. At this point it is a good idea to place the reed onto its bocal to check the fit. If the reed pushes too far onto the bocal, the shape at the butt may have been too wide. If further tightening of the bottom wire does not reduce the size of the tube, remove the wires and reshape the butt of the reed. Then reassemble the reed and recheck the fit on the bocal. If the tube is too narrow to fit far enough onto the bocal, it can be reamed out after it dries.

Allow the reed to dry completely, for at least 24 hours. The cane will shrink some during drying, so place the reed on the mandrel and retighten the wires. Trim the excess wire to about five millimeters, but do not bend the wire ends down yet. Coat the area between the lower two wires with *Duco Cement* and wrap this area with some nylon string, tying it off with a half-hitch. A ball of string can be wrapped over the bottom wire, if desired. Apply a generous coat of *Duco Cement* over the string and allow it to dry. Trim the bottom wire close to the base, leaving one or two twists to hold it in place, and bend the tips of the top wires down flat.

Wet the blades of the reed and place it on the bocal. If the reed does not fit far

Figure 6.7. Placing the wires on the folded reed.

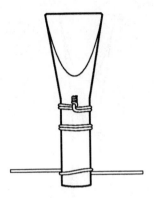

enough onto the bocal, the tube of the reed can be enlarged with a reamer or a needle file. Finally, close off the end of the bocal with your finger and blow through the reed to check for leakage around the butt of the reed. If there is any remaining leakage, work some hot beeswax (or candle wax) into the reed tube using the mandrel. The reed is now ready for final scraping.

Scraping the Reed

The scrape should satisfy three basic conditions: (1) the reed should be free-blowing and tongue easily in all registers; (2) the reed should function well acoustically to provide optimum performance and proper tuning; and (3) the reed should provide a desirable tone color. A French-style scrape is the most useful scrape for curtal reeds. This type of scrape consists of a straight taper from the beginning of the lay to the tip of the blade, as shown in Figure 6.8a. The sides of the reed are left thick, and the tip will display a crescent shape when held up to a strong light. This is represented by the dotted line in Figure 6.8b.

Begin by removing wood in the lay so that it forms a gentle taper toward the tip. Thin the tip according to the crescent shape shown in Figure 6.8b. Next, check the closing of the reed tip by gently squeezing the blades between your thumb and first finger at the point where your embouchure would be placed. (Be sure the reed has been soaked properly before performing this procedure.) The blades should touch at all points simultaneously, as in Figure 6.9a, or close last at the very center, as in Figure 6.9b. A reed which closes in one motion will produce the

Figure 6.8. Scraping the lay of the curtal reed.

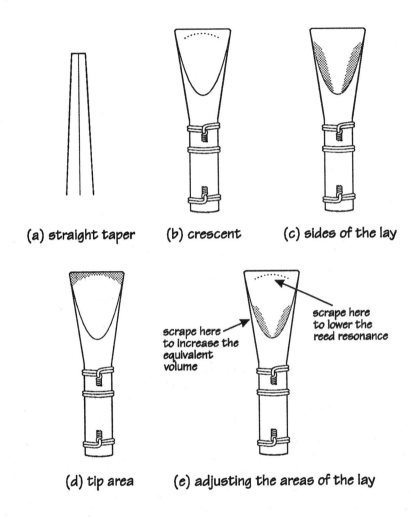

(a) straight taper   (b) crescent   (c) sides of the lay

scrape here → to increase the equivalent volume

scrape here to lower the reed resonance

(d) tip area   (e) adjusting the areas of the lay

brightest timbre, while a reed which never completely closes at the center will produce the darkest tone. Thus, a darker tone quality may be attained by leaving slightly more wood in the center at the tip and just behind the tip than at the sides. If the reed closes in the center first (Figure 6.9c), an unstable acoustic situation will occur. This type of tip closure results from the center of the blade tip being less stiff than the sides. If the corners seem too thick, thin them and recheck the tip closure. If this does not help, remove more wood along the sides of the lay (as shown in Figure 6.8c), or trim the tip and rebalance the tip opening.[6]

Figure 6.9. Checking the tip opening.

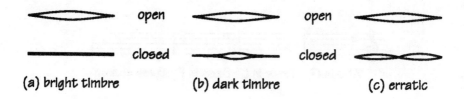

open	open	
closed	closed	
(a) bright timbre	**(b) dark timbre**	**(c) erratic**

When the tip has a desirable closure, place the reed on the bocal and sound the pitch obtained by using the same embouchure as when playing the instrument. The resultant pitch should be near the octave of the low-register note fingered 123 ————. This pitch is approximately D_5 for an alto curtal in G, G_4 for a tenor curtal in C, C_4 for the bass curtal in F, and C_4 for the bass shawm in F (see Figure 6.10). The exact reed-plus-bocal driving frequency can also be determined by using an old reed which is known to work well.

This simple diagnostic test will tell you whether the reed meets its acoustic requirements for playing the lower register in tune. If this pitch is unstable, the tip may be too open or the blades may be too thin. If the pitch is too high, the tip may be too closed, or the lay may need to be lengthened or thinned. On the other hand, if the note is too low, the tip may be too open, or the lay may need to be shortened by trimming the tip. When the proper reed-plus-bocal driving frequency can be sounded, place the setup on the instrument and play the lower octave of the instrument.

If the reed tongues poorly in the low register, thin the tip area (the shaded area in Figure 6.8d) until a good response is achieved. Proceed slowly, because if the area behind the tip becomes too thin, the reed will not respond well in the upper register. When making these adjustments, the tip opening may also change and need to be adjusted by squeezing the top wire.

Next, check the pitch of the note fingered 123 4567 by comparing it with a tuning standard. If this note is sharp, continue to thin the blades toward the back of the lay, as shown in Figure 6.8e. Then check this note with its octave. If the upper note is sharp in relation to its lower octave, the equivalent volume of the reed is too small. Continue to scrape the back of the lay until the notes of the lower register are properly tuned.

If the blades become too soft during this process, however, all pitches will become unstable, and the reed will be very difficult to overblow. If this occurs, it may be necessary to redesign the reed with a slightly longer blade length.

Now check the tuning of the first five notes of the instrument with their octaves,

Figure 6.10. Approximate reed-plus-staple driving frequencies for curtals.

Alto In G   Tenor In C   Bass In F   Bass shawm

as shown in Figure 6.11. This test helps to determine whether the reed resonance has been correctly located. If the octaves overblow flat, the reed resonance needs to be raised by shortening the blade length of the reed or by closing the tip opening slightly. Conversely, if the octaves overblow sharp, the tip opening should be increased, or the lay of the reed should be thinned at the area just behind the tip (see Figure 6.8e).[7] This is a critical area for the ability of the reed to overblow properly, so exercise caution when scraping this region. As previously stated, excessive thinning will lead to a flabby, unstable reed. Also, a tip opening that is too large may lead to an unstable situation, while a tip that is too closed will hamper the production of low notes and restrict the ability of the embouchure to make the fine adjustments to the reed resonance that are necessary for good tuning. A balance must therefore be struck between the stiffness of the blades and the size of the tip opening.

If, after adjusting the reed resonance, the equivalent volume has become mismatched to the instrument, the bocal length should be adjusted until the lower register is again properly aligned. This procedure will probably not be necessary, as the initial adjustments to the equivalent volume should also bring the reed resonance into alignment for good response in the upper register.

The actual thickness of the blades and the length of the lay will depend upon the hardness of the cane. Reeds that have been constructed from harder cane can be scraped thinner without losing stability, while reeds made from softer cane require that more wood be left on the blades and that slightly larger overall dimensions be used in order to achieve similar results. The chief advantage of using stiffer cane is that the resultant thinner reeds will produce a more responsive low register without sacrificing ease in overblowing and stability. A more strident tone is possible with thinly gouged cane, but this can be regulated by the scrape at the tip to adjust the type of tip closing. While different batches of cane will vary in stiffness, this can be controlled more closely by an appropriate gouge thickness, since the cane becomes softer and less predictable toward the center of the cane tube.

Figure 6.11. Tuning the octaves of the lower register.

Alto curtal   Tenor curtal   Bass curtal
                                                               Bass shawm

Finally, test the tuning of the different registers by comparing the lowest note of the main scale (fingered 123 4567) with its second and third octaves (i.e., F_3 and F_4 for the bass curtal and the bass shawm), as shown in Figure 6.12. Checking the tuning of the third-octave note requires knowing your instrument well enough to be able to play this note with a harmonic fingering. Good harmonic alignment in this area will ensure maximum stability in the usable range of the instrument and can be helpful in diagnosing a problem in the reed. Since the note in the third octave lies near the reed resonance, it is quite sensitive to the exact placement of the reed resonance, while the second-octave note is more dependent upon the total equivalent volume of the reed cavity and bocal for its proper tuning.[8] If the third-octave note cannot be coaxed from the instrument, the reed may be too large to allow the production of harmonics in this area. If the note is flat, the reed blades may need to be shortened. If the note is sharp, the lay should be lengthened or scraped, or both.

If the reed does not respond well in the upper register, thin the tip area (the shaded area in Figure 6.8d), being careful not to disturb the the area of the lay just behind the tip.

On a well-designed instrument, the appropriate equivalent volume for low notes and reed resonance for proper tuning of higher partials will be related, so that making adjustments to correct one parameter will also correct the other. Additionally, this relationship between the equivalent volume and the reed resonance allows one to make small changes to either parameter by embouchure adjustment for tuning purposes without resorting to extremely different embouchures for the different registers of the instrument. Thus, once you have adjusted the reed for playing the fundamental octave in tune, you will most likely also have brought the reed resonance into position for good cooperation of upper resonances.

While I do not generally subscribe to making extensive adjustments to the throat wires of the reed, these adjustments can be helpful for salvaging a reed that has been scraped too thin or for improving commercial reeds that depend

Figure 6.12. Tuning the upper register.

**Alto curtal   Tenor curtal   Bass curtal
                                    Bass shawm**

on these procedures for adjustment. A chart for making wire adjustments is given in Table VI. These adjustments are most beneficial to German-style reeds, which have a prominent center spine and whose blades have been constructed from the spongier area of the cane tube.

TABLE VI. **Wire adjustments.**

ADJUSTMENT	PRIMARY ACOUSTIC CHANGE	PERCEIVED MUSICAL CHANGE
Rounding the top wire	Opens the tip, which lowers the reed resonance and increases its flexibility	Louder; less stable; overall flatter pitch
Flattening the top wire	Closes the tip, which raises the reed resonance toward its upper limit and decreases its flexibility	Softer; more stable; sharper overall pitch; notes are difficult to lip down
Rounding the middle wire	Closes the tip and reduces the reed volume by increased transverse tension in the blades	Tip may need adjustment by rounding the top wire; favors upper-register notes; raises the pitch of the lower register, especially the left-hand notes
Flattening the middle wire	Opens the tip and increases the reed volume by decreased transverse tension in the blades	Tip may need adjustment by flattening the top wire; favors lower register notes; lowers the pitch of the lower register, especially left-hand notes

VII

CRUMHORN REEDS

The crumhorn, a cylindrically bored woodwind with a capped double reed, occupies a unique historical position in that it has no modern descendent. The crumhorn is used only in its fundamental register, and by the addition of an upper thumbhole, it has a normal range of a ninth. Since the overblown register is not employed, the reed design is somewhat simpler than the lip-controlled reeds of conically bored instruments.

Because of the high placement of the reed resonance in relationship to the playing frequencies of the usable range in cylindrical instruments, a change in the equivalent volume of the reed will affect each harmonic by a nearly equal percentage for the lower frequencies.[1] For this reason the volume requirement of the reed is somewhat less sensitive than that of a reed for a conically bored instrument. The equivalent volume of the reed-plus-staple setup can thus be adjusted by changing the cane stiffness, the reed dimensions, and the tip opening as well as by changing the length of the staple.

The reed resonance should be optimally placed (see Figure 1.19) for increased tonal stability as well. It is determined primarily by the length and stiffness of the reed blades, and it can be adjusted by the size of the tip opening and by the amount of breath pressure used during playing.

Original sources provide us with little information about the reed and staple design for crumhorns or other capped reed instruments. Mersenne's illustrations show some smaller sizes of crumhorns which have a fan-shaped reed at the top of the instrument (see Figure 7.1). For the larger sizes of crumhorns, Praetorius depicts a fan-shaped reed with a long staple (Figure 7.2). His cylindrically bored *Sordunen*, which are acoustically related to crumhorns, appear to have conical crooks and presumably detachable reeds (see Figure 8.1). The surviving tenor crumhorn reed cited by Anthony Baines is not bound to a staple and appears to have been made to fit a conical staple.[2]

Many modern crumhorn makers supply their instruments with reeds bound to a cylindrical tube in a manner similar to bagpipe reeds. Acoustically speaking, it

Figure 7.1. Crumhorns. Mersenne, *Harmonie Universelle*, 1636.

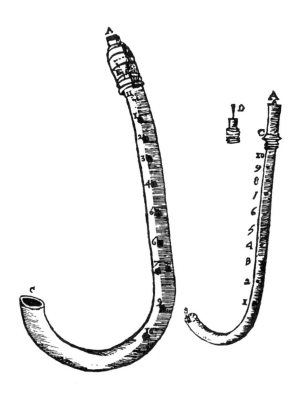

does not matter whether the staple is cylindrical or conical or whether the reed is bound to it or detachable. However, the use of a cylindrical staple can more easily lead to errors in the cane-to-staple proportions in the reed setup. This can result because it is possible to design a reed with elongated blades and a shorter staple which will play generally in tune, but the reed resonance will be placed too low to be optimally usable (see Figure 1.18). The result will be a duller timbre and unpredictable tuning. The reverse will occur if the blade length is too short and the staple is lengthened to compensate. In this situation the upper partials will be strengthened by the shift of the reed resonance, leading to "squeaking" during playing.

Since testing the reed resonance is not possible if the reed has been bound to a long staple, one must rely on playing characteristics for adjustment. If conical staples are used, the staple length will have been predetermined, and consequently upper and lower limits will have been set for an acceptable blade length. This will help to ensure that a new reed will have an appropriate reed resonance

Figure 7.2. Crumhorns. Praetorius, De Organographia, 1619.

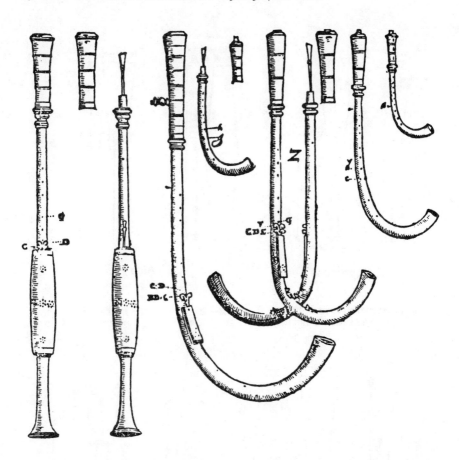

and thus simplify the reed-making process. A detachable reed can also be removed and tested directly to determine its approximate reed resonance.

Crumhorns which were designed to use plastic reeds may require some retuning in order to be retrofitted with cane reeds. Some of these instruments do not gain much from being converted to a cane-reed setup because they were designed and tuned with a specific type of plastic reed in mind. The use of plasticized bores complicates the problem even more because moisture tends to bead up and alter the shape of the air column during playing. If you are attempting to make cane reeds to replace plastic ones, be thus forewarned and be prepared to retune your instrument.[3]

The crumhorn reed designs given in Figures 7.3 and 7.4 include both bound and unbound reed styles. The bound reeds are meant to be placed on a length of cy-

Figure 7.3. Crumhorn reed measurements for reeds bound to their staples.

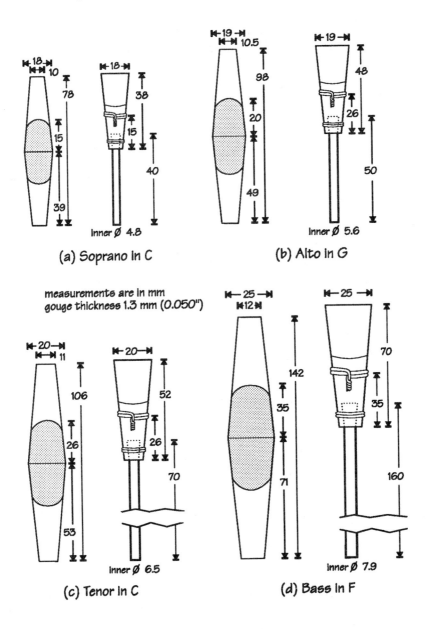

measurements are in mm
gouge thickness 1.3 mm (0.050")

(a) Soprano in C

(b) Alto in G

(c) Tenor in C

(d) Bass in F

Figure 7.4. Crumhorn reed measurements for detachable reeds.

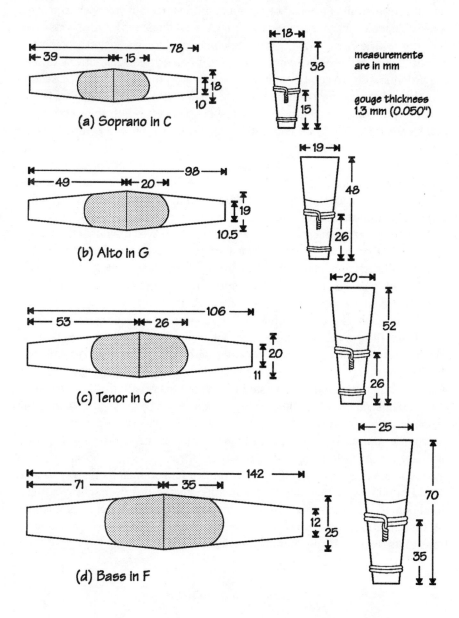

(a) Soprano in C

(b) Alto in G

(c) Tenor in C

(d) Bass in F

measurements are in mm

gouge thickness 1.3 mm (0.050")

lindrical brass tubing, while detachable reeds should be placed on conical staples. If your instrument does not have a conical staple but you wish to make a detachable reed, conical staples can be made according to the dimensions given in Figure 7.5. The exact length of the staple may need to be adjusted according to the particular bore design to which the staple is being fitted. Alternatively, the end of a cylindrical staple can be tapered by removing a thin wedge-shaped section from the end of the tube, reforming, and then silver-soldering the joint (see Figure 7.6a), or by building up the tip of the staple on the outside with some epoxy glue (see Figure 7.6b).[4] The lower end of the staple can then be wrapped with waxed string or dental floss to fit into the upper end of the instrument. Measurements have been provided for soprano, alto, tenor, and bass crumhorn reeds. For reeds that are bound to the staple, the staple lengths and the reed size may need to be adjusted according to the particular make of crumhorn being fitted and according to the reed stiffness desired.

The reed designs presented here are meant to be played dry rather than being pre-wetted. "Dry," however, does not mean cane that has been allowed to dry out completely. Reed cane retains moisture just as wood does, so that under playing conditions the cane contains a high degree of moisture but is not saturated or water-logged. The walls of a reed are softened considerably when wetted, resulting in changes in its acoustic behavior. Similarly, a reed which is completely dried out and has little or no moisture content will behave differently from one that has a high moisture content but is not saturated with water. Under playing conditions, the dry reed is subject to the high humidity of the moist air being blown through it, and it should therefore be adjusted to play optimally with this high moisture content. Finished reeds can be kept in good condition by playing the instrument regularly. If the reeds are not going to be used for a period of time, they can be stored in a controlled-humidity environment, such as the storage box described in Chapter 1. To revive a reed that has been allowed to dry out completely, air should be blown gently through the instrument for several minutes, or the reed should be placed in the controlled-humidity storage box overnight. Wetting a dried-out reed and then adjusting it for this type of moisture is not recommended because additional adjustments will be required later as the reed gradually returns to its original, highly humid condition.

Constructing the Reed

Soprano, alto, and tenor crumhorn reeds can be constructed from bassoon cane tubes, gouged cane, or extra-wide profiled cane. Bass crumhorn reeds are

Figure 7.5. Conical staples for crumhorns.

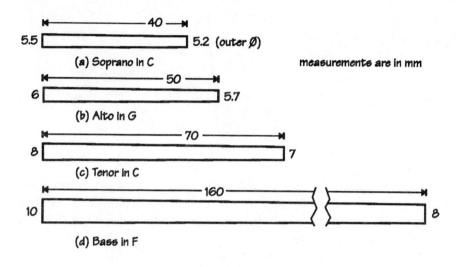

measurements are in mm

Figure 7.6. Tapering the end of a cylindrical staple.

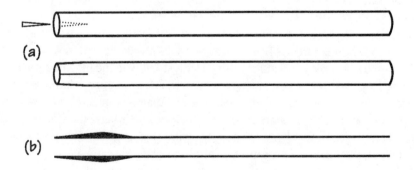

best made from contrabassoon cane. Also, dry reeds will benefit from using the spongier cane obtained from a thicker gouge. Since the cane walls are not softened by wetting, as with presoaked reeds, the tip and the lay can be left slightly thicker if the less resilient part of the cane tube is used. The gouge thicknesses of modern bassoon cane (1.3 mm, or .050") and contrabassoon cane (1.5 mm, or .060") are appropriate for these purposes. If you are gouging the cane by hand, you may want to try a slightly thicker gouge than either of these.

Figure 7.7. Crumhorn reed shape.

Cut the gouged cane to the proper length according to the given dimensions, mark the center, and profile. If you are using extra-wide profiled cane, sand the inside of the cane lightly, and cut the ends of the cane to proper length. Allow an extra two or three millimeters to be cut off the tip of this type of cane because the machine profiling is usually too thin at the tip for crumhorn reeds. Using extra-wide profiled cane for the smaller reed sizes saves time by eliminating the steps of hand gouging and profiling. Beginners will also benefit from using this type of cane in order to obtain a finished product as quickly and effortlessly as possible. Hand gouging and profiling are techniques that can be learned and then added to one's reed-making skills at a later time.

Next, fold and shape the cane. Crumhorn reeds should have a straight-sided taper, as shown in Figure 7.7. This shape combines a wide tip with a wide throat for a maximum volume of sound combined with stability in the fundamental register. The exact width of the shape at the base will depend upon the diameter of the staple. To determine this width, multiply the diameter by 3.14 and divide by two. Another method is to wrap a piece of string or wire around the staple at the point where the butt of the reed will fit. Measure this length and divide by two. For either method, allow a bit extra for shrinkage when the cane dries.

After sanding the edges of the shaped cane, unfold it and bevel the lower inside edges of the tube. Next, score the bark, refold the cane, and place two wires, as shown in Figure 7.8. A third wire placed in between these two may be used, but it is not necessary. Draw the top wire tight to prevent cracks from forming down the center of the blades.

If you are making a detachable reed, carefully work a mandrel of the proper size into the end of the reed tube to the proper depth, then tighten the butt wire. This step should be done with care so that the reed will form a tight seal with the staple. The staples of the bigger instruments are usually too large to use a mandrel

Figure 7.8. Placing the wires.

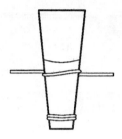

Figure 7.9. Fitting the reed to the staple.

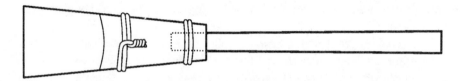

Figure 7.10. Cylindrical staple.

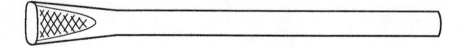

unless special ones have been made for this purpose. In this case the reed can be formed directly around the staple. Be careful that you do not collapse the staple as you tighten the bottom wire. The staple should fit into the reed only as far as the region just past the butt wire, as illustrated in Figure 7.9.

If you are binding the reed to the staple, cut a piece of cylindrical tubing to the proper length with a tube cutter or a triangular file. Squeeze one end of the staple with a pliers to make it slightly oval-shaped, as shown in Figure 7.10, and roughen the sides of this end with a file so that the cane will not slip after it has been bound onto it. Following the procedures above, work the staple into the end of the reed. (It may be easier to place the butt wire onto the reed after inserting the staple, and thus prevent the end of the staple from digging into the inside of the

Figure 7.11. Crumhorn reed tip openings.

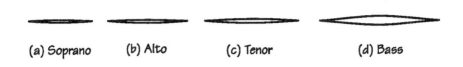

(a) Soprano   (b) Alto   (c) Tenor   (d) Bass

cane.) Tighten the butt wire so that the end of the staple fits as far into the reed
as shown in Figure 7.9.

Next, cut off the excess wire and sand the sides of the reed until they are flush.
Cut off the tip and, if necessary, adjust the top wire. The blades should appear
quite flat, so that there is a minimum of added tension to the blades. The tip
should appear to be almost entirely closed for small reeds, and progressively
more open for larger ones. Correct tip openings are illustrated in Figure 7.11. If
enough wood was removed during the profiling process, the reed should now produce a sound.

A detachable crumhorn reed can be bound with string in a manner similar to
the curtal reed. First, allow the reed to dry completely, for at least 24 hours. The
cane will shrink some during drying, so the wires should be retightened. Trim the
excess wire to about five millimeters, but do not bend the wire ends down yet.
Coat the area between the wires with *Duco Cement*, and wrap this area with some
nylon string, tying it off with a half-hitch. Apply a coat of *Duco Cement* over the
string and allow it to dry. Bend the tips of the wires down flat. Then place the reed
onto its staple and blow through the reed to check for leakage around the butt of
the reed.

If you are binding the reed to its staple, allow the reed to dry and then retighten
the wires, being sure that the bottom wire is tight and secures the reed snugly to
the staple. Trim off any excess wire. Coat the area from below the top wire down
to the beginning of the staple with *Duco Cement* and wrap the area with nylon
string. Apply a generous coat of *Duco Cement* over the string and allow it to dry.
Bend the tips of the wires down flat. Finally, check for leakage around the butt of
the reed by blowing through the reed assembly, and seal any leaks with *Duco Cement*. The reed is now ready for final scraping.

Scraping the Reed

Crumhorn reeds should be scraped thinly and evenly over the entire area of the
lay with an additional wedge-shaped cut taken out of the heart, leaving just

Figure 7.12. Scraping dry cane.

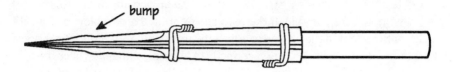

Figure 7.13. Checking the tip opening.

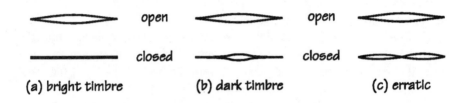

| (a) bright timbre | (b) dark timbre | (c) erratic |

enough arch so that the tip closes properly. For the larger sizes, a shoulder can be cut into the cane just above the top wire at the start of the lay, as is commonly found on modern bassoon reeds. The tip will appear thicker and much more closed than on other types of reeds.

Begin by checking the tip opening and adjust it, if necessary. Then scrape both blades, beginning from the top wire and working toward the tip. Although the blades are dry, you do not have to worry about splitting them because there is very little arch in the cane. Scraping dry cane is somewhat different from scraping wetted cane, and "bumps" are more easily formed in the lay, as shown in Figure 7.12. Try to use long knife strokes, do not work very long in the same area, and stop often to observe your work under a strong light. If you do end up with some bumps in the lay, try working them out with a flat file.

After the lay has been thinned, check the tip closing by gently squeezing the blades between the thumb and first finger. The blades should touch at all points simultaneously, as in Figure 7.13a. A reed which closes in one motion will produce the brightest timbre and will provide the most stable tone. If the tip closes last in the center (Figure 7.13b), the center area just behind the tip needs to be scraped some more. If the reed closes in the center first (Figure 7.13c), the reed will provide an acoustically unstable condition when placed on the instrument. This type of tip closure results from the sides of the blade tip being stiffer than the center. If the corners seem too thick, thin them and recheck the tip closure. If this does not help, remove more wood along the sides of the lay, or trim the tip and rebalance the tip opening until the proper tip closure is achieved.

Next, test the reed on the instrument. Adjust the tip opening as necessary until the lowest notes are playable. If the reed seems stuffy, hard to blow, or squeaks easily, continue to thin the lay and to adjust the tip opening. After the lowest notes of the instrument have been tuned correctly to a tuning standard, check the tuning of the left-hand notes. If the reed blows easily but the left-hand notes are flat compared to the right-hand notes, the reed tip should be trimmed and the lay rebalanced. If you have used a cylindrical staple and the reed sounds all right but the left-hand notes are flat, you may need to shorten the staple in order to bring these notes up to pitch. Conversely, if the reed plays well but the left-hand notes are sharp, the staple can be lengthened.

If the lowest two notes are sharp but the upper notes of the scale are correctly tuned, the equivalent volume of the reed cavity is too small. To remedy this, increase the length of the lay or continue to thin the back of the lay. If the reed blades already seem thin enough, the top wire may need to be moved back to increase the blade length. On the other hand, if the lowest two notes tend to be flat in relation to the rest of the scale, the lay should be shortened by trimming the tip and readjusting the opening.

To determine if the reed resonance is appropriately located, check the pitch of the third harmonic of the lowest note (fingered Th 123 4567) by leaking the thumbhole. (On most crumhorns the thumbhole can be used as a register hole in this fashion to sound the third harmonic of the lowest notes of the instrument. On bass crumhorns, however, the thumbhole may be too far away from an ideal acoustic placement to allow this test to function properly.) This pitch should be a twelfth above the fundamental. If this harmonic is sharp or flat, the blade length should be lengthened or shortened until the pitch is properly tuned. If the fundamental tends to be sharp in relation to the overblown note, the reed should be additionally scraped toward the back of the lay. If the fundamental tends to be flat, the reed blades may need to be narrowed slightly, or the holes may need retuning.

Generally speaking, a reed that has not been scraped enough in the lay will be more likely to squeak and may cause the lowest notes to be sharp, while a reed that has been scraped too thin will result in a less stable setup, flat left-hand notes, and sagging pitch on the cutoff of a note. After a little experience with these variables, it becomes apparent which choices to make in order to obtain the best balance for desired playing characteristics.

The tip opening can be adjusted to increase or decrease the volume of sound and to suit one's desired blowing pressure. However, the more open the tip, the more sensitive the equivalent volume is to breath pressure, so that using a reed with a larger tip opening may make the instrument less stable if a constant high breath pressure cannot be maintained. Since this can lead to unstable situations, a balance should be sought between volume of sound and pitch stability when deciding how much to open the tip. Tenor crumhorns seem to be the least adversely affected by these acoustic changes, while the sopranos are particularly sensitive to changes in the tip opening. For maximum stability, the soprano reed should be relatively stiff and quite closed, while the reeds for the larger sizes should be progressively softer and more open.

Occasionally the tip of a dry reed will warp so that it does not close correctly when it is blown, and the resultant timbre of the instrument will be noticeably dull or inconsistent. This can occur during the reed construction process if the reed has been wetted and the blades are subsequently allowed to dry unevenly. During the scraping process the tip should be left as thick as possible to help prevent this situation. However, if the tip of an otherwise correctly scraped reed has become deformed, it can be reshaped by the following procedure: (1) close the tip completely by squeezing the top wire; (2) wet the blades; (3) gently insert a contoured bassoon plaque between the blades; (4) allow the reed to dry overnight with the plaque in place; and (5) remove the plaque and readjust the tip opening via the top wire. The tip should now retain the desired type of opening.

Underblowing Technique on the Bass Crumhorn

The underblowing technique apparently referred to by Martin Agricola[5] in his woodwind fingering chart (reproduced in Figure 7.14) is an interesting phenomenon. It requires the use of a reed with a flexible equivalent volume and a properly placed reed resonance in order to operate optimally. To sound Bb_1 by fingering F_2 (see Figure 7.15), the breath pressure is reduced, causing the lower two resonances, F_2 and C_4, to sag. This reduction in pressure causes a slight lowering of the reed resonance and a large increase in the equivalent volume of the reed. Because the bore resonances that lie near the reed resonance are influenced by its position to a much greater degree than resonances that lie far below it, the relative stability of the reed resonance prevents the upper resonances of the note from being flattened as much as the fundamental when the equivalent volume of the reed is increased. Thus, F_2 moves farther in pitch than C_4, while the third resonance (A_4) moves only a small distance. The resultant regime of oscillation produces the pitch Bb_1. One can proceed upward in a similar manner, sustaining pitches that sound a fifth below the normal scale of the instrument. Since the primary stabilizing factor of the underblown note is the strength of the second air-

Figure 7.14. Woodwind fingering chart. Martin Agricola, *Musica Instrumentalis Deutsch*, 1528.

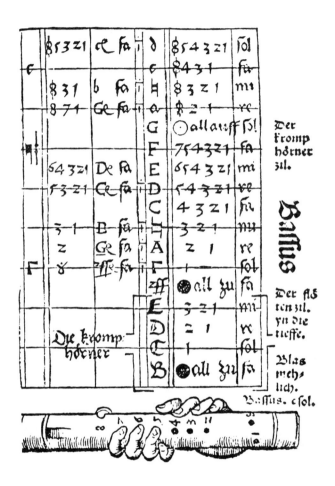

column resonance of the fingered note, a bore design with strong upper resonances will produce the most effective result when combined with an appropriate reed.

Making a bass crumhorn reed that can underblow the lowest four notes to Bb_1, C_2, D_2, and Eb_2 will require using quite thin blades and a more open tip. This setup allows for a more flexible equivalent volume, which can be manipulated by reducing one's breath pressure and thereby allow the lower pitches to sound. If the pitch will not drop or will not drop far enough when the reed is being tested,

Figure 7.15. Underblowing technique on the bass crumhorn.

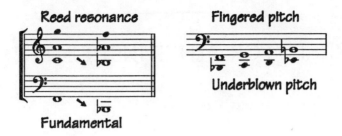

the lay should be lengthened or thinned again and the tip should be opened more. A balance must be found so that the tuning of the normal scale of the instrument is not upset. The disadvantage of this setup is that its stability relies mainly upon the strength of the upper resonances of the fingered note and the ability to maintain a constant lowered breath pressure.[6] In addition, using a reed with a very open tip requires that a high breath pressure be constantly maintained while playing in the normal range of the instrument in order to prevent the pitch from fluctuating or sagging.

VIII

REEDS FOR OTHER INSTRUMENTS

The members of the shawm, curtal, and crumhorn families represent the primary types of double-reed instruments that were used during the Renaissance. Some less well documented woodwinds are known to have existed, and many of these instruments have been reconstructed or copied by modern builders. The proliferation of these instruments in the twentieth century has perhaps distorted our perception as to how common or widespread they really were during the Renaissance. For our purposes, all these instruments can be considered variations of the crumhorn design.

Capped Reeds with a Cylindrical Bore

Acoustically speaking, the instruments of this group are essentially crumhorns. They are documented mainly by Praetorius and include the *Kortholt* (reproduced in Figure 8.1) and the *Corna-musa*. Although Praetorius did not include an illustration of the *Corna-musa*, his description of the instrument suggests that it was equivalent to a straight crumhorn, but with a covered bell and a quieter sound. The size and scrape of reeds for the *Kortholt* and the *Corna-musa* are consequently similar to the corresponding size of crumhorn reeds. Refer to Chapter 7 for details of construction.

Capped Reeds with a Conical Bore

The capped shawm employs the capped double-reed tone generator of a crumhorn coupled to the conical bore of a shawm. The *Rauschpfeife* was apparently known in Germany during the early sixteenth century (see Figure 8.2).[1] In the seventeenth century Mersenne described a similar instrument, the *hautbois de Poitou*, as having been constructed in three sizes: *dessus*, *taille*, and *basse* (see Figure 8.3).

Figure 8.1. Cylindrically bored instruments: *Kortholt* and *Sordunen*. Praetorius, *De Organographia*, 1619.

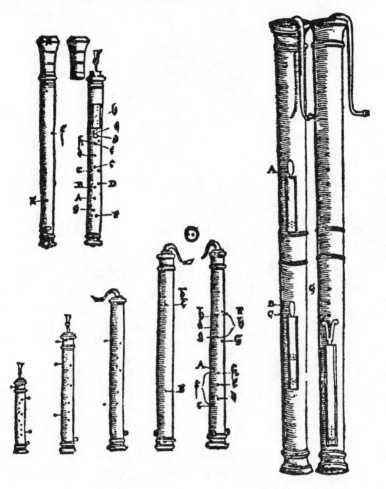

These instruments all employ a thumbhole, as on a crumhorn, and this allows a range of a ninth. Because the instruments have a conical bore, extending this range by overblowing is possible. However, considering the noticeable change in tone quality and the difficulty in controlling overblown notes with the capped-reed setup, it seems unlikely that playing in the upper register was intended.

From our knowledge of the designs of shawm reeds and crumhorn reeds, calculating the proper reed size for *Rauschpfeifen* is rather simple. Modern reproduc-

Figure 8.2. *Rauschpfeifen* from *The Triumph of Maximilian I*, c. 1508–1519.

tions are usually built in four sizes (sopranino in F, soprano in C, alto in F, and tenor in C), as shown in Figure 8.4. Since the *Rauschpfeife* has a conical bore, we can determine an appropriate reed resonance for each size from the corresponding size of shawm, as was given in Figure 1.5. Thus, the soprano *Rauschpfeife* in C should have a reed resonance of approximately D_6, the alto size should be near G_5, the tenor size should be about D_5, and the sopranino size can be estimated to be about G_6. Since these instruments are capped reeds, they will behave similarly to crumhorn reeds. After checking the reed resonances of the crumhorn reeds in Figure 1.19, it is apparent that the soprano, alto, tenor, and bass sizes of crumhorn reeds as described in Chapter 7 will closely fit the proportions of the four sizes of *Rauschpfeifen*. These dimensions have been reproduced in Figure 8.5.

Figure 8.3. *Hautbois et cornemuse de Poitou*. Mersenne, *Harmonie Universelle*, 1636.

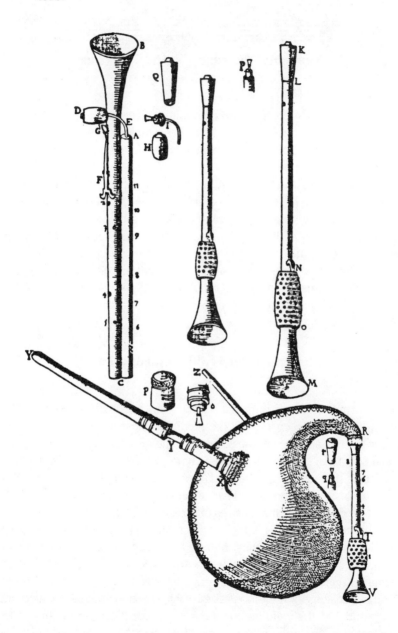

Figure 8.4. Ranges for modern *Rauschpfeifen*.

To construct reeds for the *Rauschpfeife*, follow the procedures in Chapter 7 for crumhorn reeds. Detachable reeds with conical staples are probably the most appropriate, but because of the instrument's limited range, a reed bound to a cylindrical staple may also be used.

The scrape of the lay should be quite thin, as with crumhorn reeds. The air-column resonances lie closer together on a conically bored instrument, so squeaking or creeping up octaves can be more of a problem than with a crumhorn. To remedy this, additional thinning of the lay may be necessary, and the tip may need to be slightly more open.

If you are making a cane reed for a *Rauschpfeife* that was originally equipped with a plastic reed, some retuning of the holes may be necessary. This will help to eliminate octave jumps caused by holes which are too small.

Uncapped Reeds with a Cylindrical Bore

The final group of instruments are those with cylindrical bores which are played with direct lip contact on the reed. The most commonly known instruments with such a setup are the *Sordun* and the *Rackett* (illustrated in Figures 8.1, 8.6, and 8.7). Both of these instruments have an increased range by a downward extension of the bore below the fundamental scale. Similar to the *Sordun* is the *courtaut*, an instrument described by Mersenne and reproduced in Figure 8.8.

Rackett reeds and the smaller sizes of *Sordun* reeds can be constructed like the detachable crumhorn reeds or the bound crumhorn reeds, as described in Chapter 7. (The bass *Sordun* reed must be fitted to a bocal.) Since modern reproductions of *Racketten* and *Sordunen* are seen with a variety of different reed and staple designs, it is generally preferable to copy whatever setup was originally used.

Reed dimensions for the various sizes of *Racketten* and *Sordunen* are given in Figures 8.9 and 8.10. It should be noted that these reeds are similar in size to the equivalent size of crumhorn reed, except that the blade length has been length-

Figure 8.5. Reed dimensions for modern *Rauschpfeifen*.

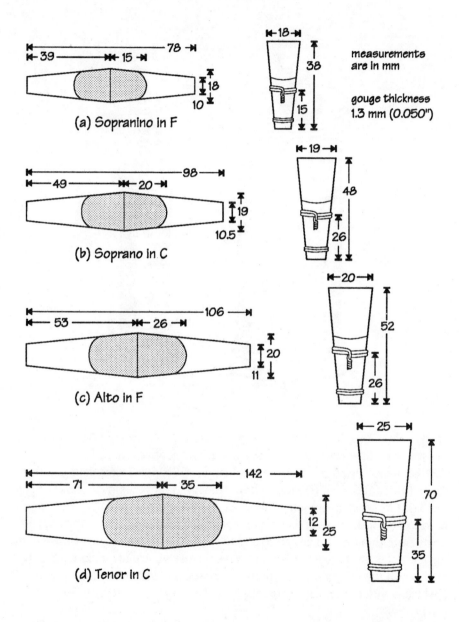

(a) Sopranino in F

measurements are in mm

gouge thickness
1.3 mm (0.050")

(b) Soprano in C

(c) Alto in F

(d) Tenor in C

Figure 8.6. *Cervelat.* Mersenne, *Harmonie Universelle,* 1636.

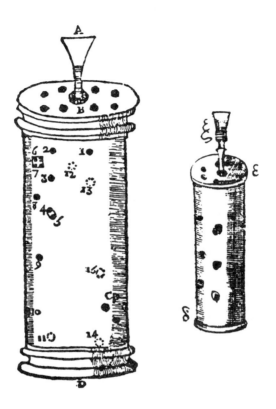

ened slightly. This allows for the use of a more tapered scrape, which increases the stability of the reed when direct embouchure control is added.

To construct the reed, follow the instructions in Chapter 7 for making crumhorn reeds. During the scraping process, taper the lay toward the tip (as shown in Figure 8.11a) rather than thinning the entire blade area (Figure 8.11b). The tip will need to be a little more open on a lip-controlled reed than on a crumhorn reed. Continue to thin the middle and back of the lay and to adjust the tip opening until the low notes are brought down into tune. Squeaking usually indicates that the reed is still too stiff or that the tip is too closed. Try to balance the thinness of the blades with the amount of tip opening. If the tip is too open, the instrument will be less stable.

The design of the *Rackett* reed may need to be altered to fit a particular pirouette design. A common problem with *Rackett* reeds is making the reed too

Figure 8.7. Cylindrically bored instruments: *Racketten*. Praetorius, *De Organographia*, 1619.

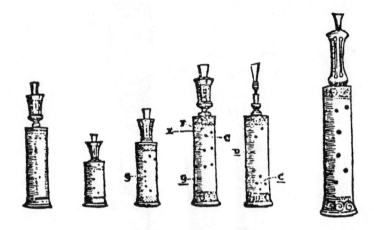

small, so that the tip must be opened up quite wide to compensate. Replacing this type of setup with a larger reed that has a slightly more closed tip will improve the pitch and stability of the instrument. If the pirouette on the *Rackett* is not adjustable, it may be necessary to alter the tube length of the reed or the staple in order to bring the appropriate area of the blades into the lip area. In this situation, start with the dimensions of an old reed and make adjustments until the desired results are obtained.

Modern reproductions of the fourteenth- and fifteenth-century *douçaine* are found both as capped reeds and as lip-controlled reeds. To make a reed for a capped *douçaine*, substitute a crumhorn reed of the equivalent size, as shown in Figures 7.3 and 7.4. For an uncapped *douçaine*, use the measurements of the appropriate size of *Sordun* reed (illustrated in Figure 8.10), and scrape accordingly.

Figure 8.8. *Courtaut* and reed. Mersenne, *Harmonie Universelle*, 1636.

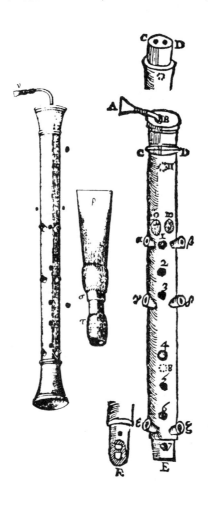

Figure 8.9. Rackett reed dimensions.

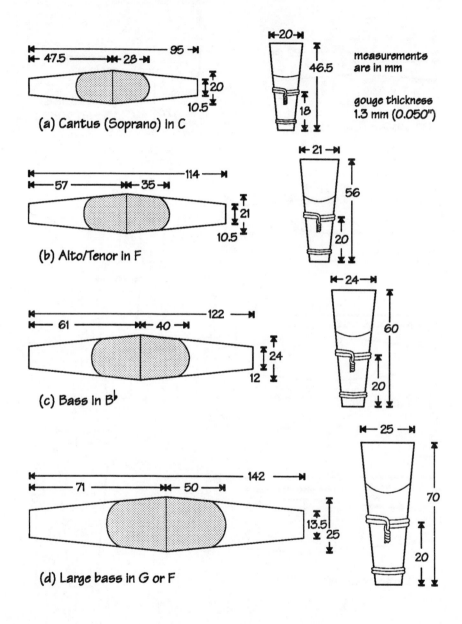

(a) Cantus (Soprano) in C

(b) Alto/Tenor in F

(c) Bass in B♭

(d) Large bass in G or F

measurements are in mm

gouge thickness 1.3 mm (0.050")

Figure 8.10. *Sordun* reed dimensions.

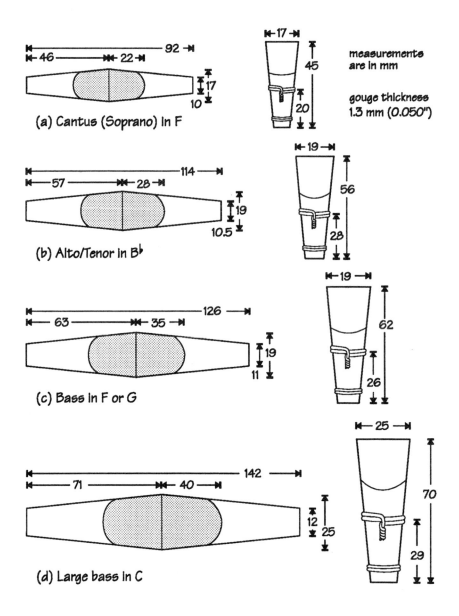

measurements
are in mm

gouge thickness
1.3 mm (0.050")

(a) Cantus (Soprano) in F

(b) Alto/Tenor in B♭

(c) Bass in F or G

(d) Large bass in C

Figure 8.11. Capped and uncapped reed-scraping styles for
                cylindrically bored instruments.

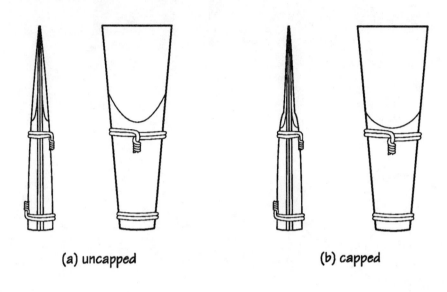

       (a) uncapped   **(b) capped**

APPENDIX

Mail-Order Reed-Making Supplies

Tube cane, gouged cane, and reed-making supplies:

Peter Angelo
P. O. Box 4005
Greenwich, CT 06830

Christlieb Products
3311 Scadlock Lane
Sherman Oaks, CA 91403
(818) 783–6554

Double Reed Shop
P. O. Box 374
Grand Haven, MI 49417
(616) 842–6832

Forrest's Music
1849 University Avenue
Berkeley, CA 94703
(510) 845–7178

Keith E. Loraine
787 Liberty Rd.
Petaluma, CA 94952
(707) 763–3981

Edmund Nielsen
Woodwind Instrument Service
53 E. St. Charles Rd.
Villa Park, IL 60181
(312) 833–5676

Jack Spratt Woodwind Shop
11 Park Avenue, P. O. Box 277
Old Greenwich, CT 06870

Gail Warnaar, Double Reeds
P. O. Box 374
Grand Haven, MI 49417
(616) 842–6832

Oilstones, slipstones, gouges, and miscellaneous tools:

Constantine
2050 Eastchester Road
Bronx, NY 10461
(800) 223–8087

Woodcraft
210 Wood County Industrial Park
P. O. Box 1686
Parkersburg, WV 26102–1686
(800) 225–1153

Tube cane:

François Alliaud
224 rue de la République
F-84310 Morières-les-Avignon
France

Dante Biasotto
Route de Boron 83
Fréjus, France

Albert Glotin
15, rue du Progrès
95460 Ezanville
France

NOTES

Introduction

1. Johann Joachim Quantz, *Versuch einer Anweisung die Flöte traversiere zu spielen* (Berlin, 1752); edited and translated by Edward R. Reilly as *On Playing the Flute* (New York: Schirmer, 1975), pp. 85–86.

2. For a history and a compositional analysis of *Arundo donax*, see Robert E. Perdue, Jr., "*Arundo donax*—Source of Musical Reeds and Industrial Cellulose," *Economic Botany* 12 (1958), pp. 368–404.

3. Ibid., p. 391.

4. See Anthony Baines, *Woodwind Instruments and Their History*, 3d ed. (New York: W. W. Norton, 1967), pp. 88–89.

I. Acoustics

1. For a text on musical acoustics that is generally regarded as the most accessible and nontechnical for musicians, see Arthur Benade, *Fundamentals of Musical Acoustics* (New York: Oxford University Press, 1976).

2. An exception is the lowest note of the bassoon and the curtal, which is obtained by closing all the holes in the bell section with the thumbs.

3. Arthur Benade, "On Woodwind Instrument Bores," *Journal of the Acoustical Society of America* 31 (1959), pp. 137–139.

4. Praetorius describes some other less familiar instruments, including the *Bassanello*, the *Corna-musa*, the *Kortholt*, and the *Schryari*. The *Bassanello* was a deep-pitched, conically bored instrument, while the *Corna-musa*, the *Kortholt*, and the *Schryari* appear to have been acoustically similar in bore and reed design to the crumhorn.

5. Benade, *Fundamentals*, p. 439.

6. For a more thorough examination of this topic, see ibid., pp. 447–462.

7. Ibid., pp. 449–450.

8. Ibid., pp. 484, 486.

9. Arthur Benade and W. Bruce Richards, "Oboe normal mode adjustment via reed and staple proportioning," *Journal of the Acoustical Society of America* 73 (1983), p. 1795.

10. Ibid., p. 1795.

11. Baroque oboes and bassoons also have a similar cutoff frequency.

12. For a more thorough discussion of adjusting the size and placement of tone holes on early woodwinds, see Herbert W. Myers, "The Practical Acoustics of Early Woodwinds," Stanford University D. M. A. Final Project, 1980, pp. 8–24.

13. Arthur Benade, "Measured end corrections for woodwind tone holes," *Journal of the Acoustical Society of America* 41 (1967), p. 1609.

14. Benade, *Fundamentals*, p. 449.

15. Ibid., p. 436.

16. Arthur Benade and J. M. Gebler, "Reed cavity and neck proportions in conical woodwinds," *Journal of the Acoustical Society of America* 55 (1974), p. 458; Benade, *Fundamentals*, p. 461.

17. Benade, *Fundamentals*, p. 471. Although changes to the equivalent volume of the reed have a greater effect on upper-bore modes than lower ones, the modes which lie nearer the

reed resonance are strongly influenced by its presence. The net result under playing conditions is that the lower resonances which support a tone actually move more easily than the upper ones when the reed volume is altered and the reed resonance is left unchanged.

18. Benade, "Oboe normal mode adjustment," p. 1796.

19. Benade, *Fundamentals*, pp. 465–470. This method of calculation can be helpful when designing reeds for unusual bore designs, or to help determine whether the staple size should be changed. The formula is based on the design of Bessel horns (see ibid., pp. 408–409).

20. In the case of the modern Viennese oboe and the modern conservatory-system oboe, the joint playing frequency lies somewhat higher, at approximately C_6. Also, for a variety of reasons the modern conservatory-system oboe is designed to be played with a varying joint playing frequency so that its lowest notes (below D_4) must be lipped down somewhat to be played in tune. Deviations from exact conicity of the bore may require a slightly different joint playing frequency for various instrument designs (see Benade, "Oboe normal mode adjustment," p. 1797; *Fundamentals*, pp. 467–469).

21. Benade, "Oboe normal mode adjustment," pp. 1798–1801.

22. Stephen C. Thompson, "The effect of the reed resonance on woodwind tone production," *Journal of the Acoustical Society of America* 66 (1979), p.1304. Thompson's work is based on the study of the reed resonance of a modern clarinet reed. My own experiments and experience in reed making suggest that double reeds for early woodwinds are the most flexible yet stable when the reed resonance can similarly be manipulated over a range of about a fifth. If fluctuations larger than this are possible by normal embouchure adjustments and blowing pressure, the reed will be less stable and will be perceived as being too "soft" or having a tip that is too open. This is consistent with Cooper's findings for the modern bassoon reed. See Lewis Hugh Cooper, "Reed Contribution," *The Double Reed* 13 (No. 3, Winter 1990), pp. 66–67.

23. Benade, *Fundamentals*, p. 436; Cornelis J. Nederveen, *Acoustical Aspects of Woodwind Instruments* (Amsterdam: Frits Knuf, 1969), p. 43.

24. Benade, "Reed Cavity and Neck Proportions," p. 458.

· 25. Benade, "Oboe normal mode adjustment," pp. 1799–1801.

26. Ibid., p. 1801.

27. Ibid., p. 1798.

28. Frederick W. Westphal, *Guide to Teaching Woodwinds* (Dubuque: Wm. C. Brown Co., 1962), pp. 119–125, 159–162.

29. Nederveen, *Acoustical Aspects*, p. 92.

30. Arthur Benade, "On the Tone Color of Wind Instruments," *Selmer Bandwagon* 59 (1969), p. 21. Backus has concluded that the particular shape of the mouth and throat cavities of the player has little appreciable effect on the tone quality produced by a woodwind instrument. (See John Backus, "The effect of the player's vocal tract on woodwind instrument tone," *Journal of the Acoustical Society of America* 78 [July 1985], p. 20.) Changes in the focus and speed of the air stream are probably responsible for the perceived tonal changes caused by alterations in the shape of the mouth and throat while playing rather than by any actual resonant effects in these areas.

31. Benade, *Fundamentals*, p. 447.

32. This terminology is derived from reed styles associated with modern German and French bassoon playing. The modern Heckel-style bassoon reed combines a strong center spine for the stability of the reed parameters coupled with thin sides all the way back to a notched "collar" at the top wire. By using a thicker gouge, the spongier area from inside the cane tube can be used. This type of reed is physically small enough to push the upper range of the bassoon yet acoustically "flabby" enough to allow cooperation with the lowest register. Since the spine also aids in maintaining the tip opening, the German scrape is

less sensitive to alterations in embouchure formation than the French scrape and tends to require less maintenance as the cane ages.

33. Benade, *Fundamentals*, p. 451; Myers, "Practical Acoustics," pp. 20–21. While this phenomenon is well known to musicians, it has not yet been subject to scientific scrutiny, and the exact mechanism remains unclear.

34. For example, the standard modern fingering for $C\sharp_3$ requires the awkward addition of the low D key with the left thumb.

35. Michael Praetorius, *Syntagma Musicum* II: *De Organographia* (Wolfenbüttel, 1619), Plate XI (reproduced in Figure 5.1).

36. The shawm has an unbroken tradition up to the twentieth century, as seen in the modern Catalan shawm (see Baines, *Woodwind Instruments*, pp. 114–115). The modern bassoon has evolved from this design via the curtal and the Baroque bassoon. The production of its lowest notes (below F_2) is equivalent to closing the vent holes in the bell of a shawm. It should also be noted that the initial changes between the treble shawm and the Baroque oboe were mainly in the length of the bell section and in the size of the tone holes (see Bruce Haynes, "Lully and the rise of the oboe as seen in works of art," *Early Music* XVI [August 1988], pp. 325–326). By using a similar bore shape but reducing the bell length to a half step below the main scale, reducing the tone-hole size, and moving toward a narrower, straight-sided reed in order to make upper register playing easier and a pirouette unnecessary, a much quieter instrument evolved to suit the changing musical needs of the time.

37. For a detailed discussion, see Benade, *Fundamentals*, pp. 447–455.

38. While the note fingered 123 ———— is not particularly sensitive to the exact placement of the reed resonance, the pitch of the note above (fingered 12– –––––) is easily altered by changing the reed parameters. This phenomenon occurs because at this point in the scale there is one less bore resonance to provide stability. The reed resonance thus exerts a greater influence in the regime of oscillation and will directly affect the pitch of this note. (This characteristic is in fact common to all early woodwinds for the low-register note fingered 12– ––––.) A reed with ill-matched or extremely flexible parameters can cause the interval between these two notes to vary from its correct tuning by a considerable degree.

39. The "extended" tenor shawm and the bass shawm, as depicted by Praetorius, have bell sections that extend a fourth below their main scale. These instruments therefore resemble the treble shawm in design but have extension keys that allow the holes in the bell section to be closed.

40. Benade, *Fundamentals*, p. 480.

41. This is illustrated by Myers through the image of gradually opening a cylindrical bore with a series of full-length straight-sided reamers having successively wider tapers until the bore modes have been compressed into a relationship resembling the harmonic series. See Myers, "Practical Acoustics," pp. 30–31.

42. This storage method is adapted from Ronald H. Orcutt and William A. Roscoe, "Reed Storage—A Simple Solution," *Journal of the International Double Reed Society* 3 (1975), pp. 31–32.

2. Embouchure Techniques

1. For more details about the scrape of the modern French bassoon reed, see Gerald Corey, "How to Make the French Bassoon 'Work,' " *Journal of the International Double Reed Society* 1 (1973), pp. 34–39.

2. Some bassoonists will make a special reed with shorter blades if they are playing passages entirely in the upper register. Also, in producing the pitch G_5 by placing the teeth directly on the reed, the reed resonance is raised to its extreme in order to allow that note to sound.

3. For an excellent description of the modern oboe embouchure, see David A. Ledet, *Oboe Reed Styles* (Bloomington: Indiana University Press, 1981), pp. 26–32.

4. In the eighteenth century, biting down on the bassoon reed was considered ill advised by Cugnier, Ozi, Quantz, and Frölich, more for the sake of tone quality rather than for pitch adjustment. See Harold Eugene Griswold, "Fundamentals of bassoon playing as described in late eighteenth-century tutors," *Journal of the International Double Reed Society* 13 (1985), pp. 35–36.

5. This may in fact actually be related to the twentieth-century trend of employing a brighter sound for orchestral playing. While Westphal recommends placing the reed into the mouth "until the upper lip is almost touching the first wire," Weissenborn (in the late nineteenth century) advised one to "lay the lips over the teeth and put the reed between the lips up to a point about 3/8 of an inch from the wire." The illustration of his reed has a blade length of 28 millimeters, which is comparable to the blade length of modern-day reeds (see Westphal, *Guide to Teaching Woodwinds*, p. 160; and Julius Weissenborn, *Fagott-Schule* [1887], translated and revised by Fred Bettoney as *Method for Bassoon* [Boston: Cundy-Bettoney Co., Inc., 1950], pp. 3–6). In his 1787 tutor, Ozi recommended that the lips be placed two to three *lignes* (4.5 to 6.8 mm) from the first wire, depending on which register was being played. According to Ozi, placing too much reed in the mouth "might result in the player's jerking the tones and would prevent him from using his tongue advantageously" (see Griswold, "Fundamentals of bassoon playing," p. 35).

6. For a listing of iconographic sources depicting shawm bands in the Renaissance, see Herbert Myers, "The Musical Resources of the Fifteenth-Century Shawm Band," Stanford University D. M. A. Term Project, 1980, pp. 57–64; see also Edmund A. Bowles, *Musical Ensembles in Festival Books 1500–1800: An Iconographical & Documentary Survey* (Ann Arbor, MI: UMI Research Press, 1989).

7. This kind of sound can be produced on modern double-reed woodwinds, but it is not considered good tone production by today's standards. See Westphal, *Guide to Teaching Woodwinds*, pp. 123–125.

8. Ibid., pp. 119–125, 159–162.

3. Reed-Making Tools

1. These illustrations have been reproduced in Figures 3.1–3.6. For an excellent summary of written accounts of eighteenth-century reed making, see Bruce Haynes, "Double reeds, 1660–1830: A survey of surviving written evidence," *Journal of the International Double Reed Society* 12 (1984), pp. 14–33. Frölich's reed-making instructions were translated and augmented from Ozi's treatise. See Harold Eugene Griswold, "Reed-Making 'Etienne Ozi (1754–1813),'" *Journal of the International Double Reed Society* 9 (1981), pp. 17–25. For a translation of Almenraeder's reed-making instructions, see "On the Making of Bassoon Reeds," *Journal of the International Double Reed Society* 8 (June, 1980), pp. 23–27.

2. For information about making hand tools, see Alexander Weygers, *The Making of Tools* (New York: Van Nostrand Reinhold Co., 1973); and Keith Loraine, *A Handbook on Making Double Reeds for Early Winds* (Berkeley, Ca.: Musica Sacra et Profana, 1982), pp. 36–41.

3. These directions are for a right-handed person. To sharpen a left-handed knife, simply reverse the instructions.

4. Constructing a Double Reed

1. Bassoon cane "profiled extra wide" is available from Edmund Nielsen Woodwind Instrument Service in Chicago. The address is given in the Appendix.

2. See Edwin Lacy, "An Experiment in Treatment of *Arundo Donax*," *Journal of the International Double Reed Society* 16 (July 1988), pp. 99–102.

3. See Marvin P. Feinsmith, "Cane Shrinkage, and an Urgent Case for the Hand-shaping

of Bassoon and Contrabassoon Reeds," *Journal of the International Double Reed Society* 14 (July 1986), p. 67.

4. Edmund Nielsen supplies gouged bassoon cane in three different thicknesses: 1.3 mm, 1.2 mm, and 1.1 mm.

5. See Griswold, "Reed-Making," p. 19; and Peter Hedrick, "Henri Brod on the Making of Oboe Reeds," *Journal of the International Double Reed Society* 6 (1978), p. 9.

6. See Paul White, "Early Bassoon Reeds: A Survey of Some Important Examples," *Journal of the American Musical Instrument Society* X (1984), pp. 74, 78–96; Geoffrey Burgess and Peter Hedrick, "The Oldest English Oboe Reeds? An Examination of Nineteen Surviving Examples," *Galpin Society Journal* XLII (August 1989), pp. 32–69.

7. This was described by Ozi and Frölich. See Griswold, "Reed-Making," p. 19.

8. Frölich recommended making a pattern from "a good reed or of parchment, sheet brass, or cardboard" (ibid., p. 21).

9. Another simple method for mounting the shaper blade is to fashion a handle from a four-inch length of brass tubing. Insert the finished shaper blade into the tubing and crimp the end of the tube flat to hold the blade in place. Finally, cover the handle with some heat-shrinkable tubing.

10. Historical reeds usually have two wires placed close together at the center and no wire at the butt. See White, "Early Bassoon Reeds," pp. 74–75, 78–96.

11. Ozi described a single iron ring at the center of the reed in the first edition of his tutor (1787), but in the second edition (1803) he showed two wires placed at the center of the reed.

12. This procedure is described by Brod in connection with making oboe reeds: "It is necessary to take care to cut the corners . . . , so that they will not prick the tongue when one releases the sound" (see Hedrick, "Henri Brod," p. 10).

13. Perdue, "*Arundo donax*," pp. 371–372.

14. See Corey, "How to Make the French Bassoon 'Work,' " p. 35.

15. See White, "Early Bassoon Reeds," pp. 70–73.

5. Shawm Reeds

1. One possible exception is the alto shawm pirouette in the *Kunsthistorisches Museum*, Vienna. A photograph of it appears in Baines, *Woodwind Instruments*, Plate XXII; detailed measurements are supplied by Myers in "Practical Acoustics," p. 106.

2. See Myers, "Musical Resources," pp. 2–4.

3. Ibid., p. 13. Praetorius gives D_1 to B_1 as the range of the treble shawm.

4. Marin Mersenne, *Harmonie Universelle* (Paris, 1636), p. 295. The treble shawm in this illustration has no pirouette, but in a different illustration (see Figure 5.3) both sizes are depicted with pirouettes.

5. See, for example, *Allegory of Hearing*, by Jan Brueghel the Elder, in Emanuel Winternitz, *Musical Instruments and their Symbolism in Western Art* (New York: W. W. Norton, 1967), Plate 37a (detail); *Itinerant Musicians Brawling*, by Georges de la Tour, in David Munrow, *Instruments of the Middle Ages and Renaissance* (London: Oxford University Press, 1976), p. 41 (detail); and *Garden of Earthly Delights*, by Hieronymus Bosch, in Robert Wangermée, *Flemish Music and Society in the Fifteenth and Sixteenth Centuries*, translated by Robert Erich Wolf (New York: Prager, 1968), Plate 77 (detail). The shawm depicted by Bosch is of alto design, and an extra reed is shown dangling from the pirouette.

6. Anthony Baines, "James Talbot's Manuscript: I. Wind Instruments," *Galpin Society Journal* 1 (1948), p. 12. Talbot's measurements are given in feet (f.), inches ('), and eighth parts of an inch ("). The measurements referring to shawm reeds, pirouettes, and staples are as follows: *English Hautbois or Waits Treble.* Height of Fliew, 1'1". Its Diametre at top, 1'3".

Length of Brass Staple, 2'3" (whereof 1'1" 1/2 inserted into the Bore of Instrt. 1'1" 1/2 into Fliew). In the Fliew at top a Hole (4" dia. 2" deep) to open a way for the passage of the Staple through the Reed: Dia. of Staple at top 1/10', at bottom 1/5'. Length of Reed, 1'1" 1/2 whereof 2" inserted into the Fliew's hole at top: breadth at top 3" 2/3. Dia. of reed at bottom 1". *Waits Tenor.* Length of Fliew, 2'. Dia. at top, 2'; of hole receiving reed 3" (whose depth 2"). Length of Reed, 1'3"; breadth at top, 3" 1/2. Dia below 1" + ; insertion, 2". Length of Staple, 3'2", whereof 1' inserted into head of Instrt. Dia. above 1/10', below 2".

7. Anthony Baines, "Shawms of the Sardana Coblas," *Galpin Society Journal* 5 (1952), pp. 9–16. See also Baines, *Woodwind Instruments*, Plate XIX, nos. 5 and 6.

8. Baines terms the shawm with a long bell section a "band shawm," being developed from the Arabo-Persian *surna* and having a detachable reed and pirouette. He terms the shawm with a short bell section a "folk shawm," being derived from the bagpipe family and having its reed bound to the staple, without a pirouette. See Baines, *Woodwind Instruments*, p. 230.

9. Loraine has compiled a table of reed dimensions of this type, including reeds for Moeck and Körber instruments. See Loraine, *Handbook*, pp. 34–35.

10. Garnier described this phenomenon in his eighteenth-century oboe tutor when he advised tuning the middle register C_5 of the oboe by comparing its pitch with the octave above (C_6) and then pushing the staple in or pulling it out accordingly. (See Thomas Warner, "Two Late Eighteenth Century Instructions for Making Double Reeds," *Galpin Society Journal* 15 [1962], p. 29.) In this situation, Garnier has assumed that the reed has been correctly proportioned (and therefore has an appropriate reed resonance). An adjustment to the position of the staple in the instrument will then have a greater effect on the pitch of middle-register notes (i.e., C_5) than on frequencies nearer the reed resonance (C_6 in this case). Whereas adjustments to the lay and the tip of the reed can affect both the equivalent volume and the reed resonance, Garnier's method of adjustment allows the equivalent volume of the reed-plus-staple setup to be adjusted without changing the reed resonance. This adjustment parameter has unfortunately been eliminated on many reproduction instruments by the use of cylindrical staple sockets, as shown in Figure 1.11a.

6. Curtal Reeds

1. Eighteenth-century reed-making sources are discussed in Chapter 3.

2. The second edition of Ozi's tutor, *Nouvelle Méthode de basson*, appeared in 1803. For commentaries, see Haynes, "Double reeds, 1660–1830," pp. 14–33; Griswold, "Reed-Making 'Etienne Ozi,'" pp. 17–25; and White, "Early Bassoon Reeds," pp. 75–77.

3. The Paris *ligne* in Ozi's time was equivalent to 2.2558290623 mm (see Griswold, "Reed-Making 'Etienne Ozi,'" p. 18). Warner incorrectly stated Ozi's gouge thickness as being half a millimeter rather than half a *ligne* ("Two Late Eighteenth Century Instructions," p. 31).

4. The illustration in the first edition (1787) of Ozi's tutor shows this single band, while the second edition (1803) shows two wires (see Figure 6.1).

5. See White, "Early Bassoon Reeds," pp. 78–96.

6. If you prefer making a reed with a long center spine, similar to the German-style scrape, adjust the tip area so that it closes in the manner of a French-style reed (Figure 6.9a).

7. Ozi and Frölich described similar final adjustments to Baroque bassoon reeds. Frölich states: "If the high range is weak, remove cane from the front with a sharp knife; if the low range is weak, shave from the back, but always with care. If it is too hard to blow it usually is because of too much arch; here it helps to press the first band together a little. If the reed produces dull tones, . . . this is helped by shaving a little from both sides or if it

is believed to be too thick remove some of the bark as already mentioned." (Griswold, "Reed-making 'Etienne Ozi,' " p. 24.) Thus, thinning the tip improves the attack of high notes, and scraping the back of the lay or lengthening the lay increases the equivalent volume of the reed for improved response in the lower register. Flattening the top wire removes tension from the blades to make it more freeblowing.

8. See Chapter 5, note 10.

7. Crumhorn Reeds

1. Benade, Fundamentals, p. 472. This is discussed in more detail in Chapter 1.

2. See Baines, Woodwind Instruments, Plate XXII.

3. Myers offers some helpful suggestions for modifying a Körber bass crumhorn for use with a cane-reed setup. See Myers, "Practical Acoustics," pp. 102–103.

4. Ibid., p. 96.

5. Martin Agricola, Musica Instrumentalis Deutsch (Wittenberg, 1529), f. ix'. This fingering chart was changed in the 1545 edition, in which the crumhorn range is given as F_2 to G_3.

6. The success of the underblowing technique varies according to the particular design used by modern crumhorn makers because of the size of the bore and the finger holes. It seems doubtful that this technique was actually widely employed by musicians of the Renaissance in view of the difficulty of controlling the pitch of the underblown notes and the fact that these notes have a different tone quality from that of the main scale of the instrument. Many bass crumhorns of this period were fitted with extension keys on the bell section to increase the lower range of the instrument, providing an acoustically more stable solution.

8. Reeds for Other Instruments

1. The term Rauschpfeife occurs in the descriptive text of the triumphal procession of Maximilian I. See Stanley Appelbaum, editor and translator, The Triumph of Maximilian I (reprint, New York: Dover, 1964), p. 9 and Plate 79.

BIBLIOGRAPHY

Agricola, Martin. *Musica instrumentalis deutsch*. Wittenberg: Georg Rhaw, 1529; 4th ed., 1545. Facsimile, Leipzig: Breitkopf & Härtel, 1896.

Almenraeder, Carl. "On the Making of Bassoon Reeds." Translated by Ester Froese and edited by Gerald Corey. *Journal of the International Double Reed Society* 8 (June 1980), pp. 23–27.

Appelbaum, Stanley, editor and translator. *The Triumph of Maximilian I*. New York: Dover, 1964.

Artley, Joe. *How to Make Double Reeds*. Stamford, CT: Jack Spratt Music Co., 1961.

Backus, John. *The Acoustical Foundations of Music*. New York: W. W. Norton, 1969.

————. "The effect of the player's vocal tract on woodwind instrument tone." *Journal of the Acoustical Society of America* 78 (July 1985), pp. 17–20.

Baines, Anthony. "James Talbot's Manuscript: I. Wind Instruments." *Galpin Society Journal* I (1948), pp. 9–26.

————. "Shawms of the Sardana Coblas." *Galpin Society Journal* V (1952), pp. 9–16.

————. *Woodwind Instruments and Their History*. 3d ed. New York: W. W. Norton, 1967.

Benade, Arthur. *Fundamentals of Musical Acoustics*. New York: Oxford University Press, 1976.

————. *Horns, Strings, and Harmony*. Garden City, NY: Doubleday, 1960.

————. "Measured end corrections for woodwind tone holes." *Journal of the Acoustical Society of America* 41 (1967), p. 1609.

————. "On the mathematical theory of woodwind finger holes." *Journal of the Acoustical Society of America* 32 (1960), pp. 1591–1608.

————. "On the Tone Color of Wind Instruments." *Selmer Bandwagon* 59 (1969), pp. 17–21.

————. "On woodwind instrument bores." *Journal of the Acoustical Society of America* 31 (1959), pp. 137–146.

————. "The Physics of Woodwinds." *Scientific American* 203 (October 1960), pp. 145–154. Reprinted in *The Physics of Music*, edited by Carleen Maley Hutchins. San Francisco: W. H. Freeman and Co., 1978.

————, and J. M. Gebler, "Reed cavity and neck proportions in conical woodwinds." *Journal of the Acoustical Society of America* 55 (1974), p. 458.

————, and P. L. Hoejke, "Vocal tract effects in wind instrument regeneration." *Journal of the Acoustical Society of America* 71 (Supplement 1, 1982), p. 591.

————, and W. Bruce Richards. "Oboe normal mode adjustment via reed and staple proportioning." *Journal of the Acoustical Society of America* 73 (1983), pp. 1794–1803.

Bowles, Edmund A. *Musical Ensembles in Festival Books 1500–1800: An Iconographical & Documentary Survey*. Ann Arbor, MI: UMI Research Press, 1989.

Boydell, Barra. *The Crumhorn and Other Renaissance Windcap Instruments*. Buren: Frits Knuf, 1982.

Bragard, Roger. *Musical Instruments in Art and History*. New York: Viking Press, 1968.

Brod Henri. *Méthode pour le hautbois*. Paris: Dufaut & Dubois, c. 1826.

Burgess, Geoffrey, and Peter Hedrick. "The Oldest English Oboe Reeds? An Examination of Nineteen Surviving Examples." *Galpin Society Journal* XLII (August 1989), pp. 32–69.

Cooper, Lewis Hugh. "Reed Contribution." *The Double Reed* 13 (No. 3, Winter 1990), pp. 59–68.

Corey, Gerald. "How to Make the French Bassoon 'Work.' " *Journal of the International Double Reed Society* 1 (1973), pp. 34–39.

Diderot, D. and J. le Rond d'Alembert. *Encyclopédie*. Paris, 1751. *Receuil de Planches*. Paris, 1765.

Frölich, Joseph. *Vollständige theoretisch-praktische Musikschule*. Bonn, 1810–11.

Garnier, J. F. *Méthode raisonnée pour le hautbois*. Paris: Pleyel, c. 1800.

Griswold, Harold Eugene. "Fundamentals of Bassoon Playing as Described in Late Eighteenth-century Tutors." *Journal of the International Double Reed Society* 13 (1985), pp. 33–41.

———. "Reed-Making 'Etienne Ozi (1754–1813).' " *Journal of the International Double Reed Society* 9 (1981), pp. 17–25.

Haynes, Bruce. "Double reeds, 1660–1830: A survey of surviving written evidence." *Journal of the International Double Reed Society* 12 (1984), pp. 14–33.

———. "Lully and the rise of the oboe as seen in works of art." *Early Music* XVI (August 1988), pp. 324–338.

———. "Making Reeds for the Baroque Oboe," I, II. *Early Music* IV (1976), pp. 31–34, 173–179.

Hedrick, Peter. "Henri Brod on the Making of Oboe Reeds." *Journal of the International Double Reed Society* 6 (1978), pp. 7–12.

Lacy, Edwin. "An Experiment in Treatment of *Arundo Donax*." *Journal of the International Double Reed Society* 16 (July 1988), pp. 99–102.

Langwill, Lindsay. *The Bassoon and Contrabassoon*. New York: W. W. Norton, 1965.

Ledet, David A. *Oboe Reed Styles*. Bloomington: Indiana University Press, 1981.

Loraine, Keith. *A Handbook on Making Double Reeds for Early Winds*. Berkeley, Ca.: Musica Sacra et Profana, 1982. Available from the author: 787 Liberty Rd., Petaluma CA 94952.

Marcuse, Sibyl. *Musical Instruments: A Comprehensive Dictionary*. New York: W. W. Norton, 1975.

Mersenne, Marin. *Harmonie Universelle*. Paris, 1636. Facsimile, Paris: Centre national de la recherche scientifique, 1975.

Meyer, Kenton Terry. *The Crumhorn: Its History, Design, Repertory, and Technique*. Ann Arbor, MI: UMI Research Press, 1983.

Munrow, David. *Instruments of the Middle Ages and Renaissance*. London: Oxford University Press, 1976.

Myers, Herbert W. "The Musical Resources of the Fifteenth-Century Shawm Band." Stanford University D. M. A. Term Project, 1980.

———. "The Practical Acoustics of Early Woodwinds." Stanford University D. M. A. Final Project, 1980.

Nederveen, Cornelis J. *Acoustical Aspects of Woodwind Instruments*. Amsterdam: Frits Knuf, 1969.

Neumann, Gayle Stuwe. *Making Double Reeds for Renaissance Woodwinds*. Available from the author: P. O. Box 32, Lafayette OR 97127.

Orcutt, Ronald H., and William A. Roscoe. "Reed Storage—A Simple Solution." *Journal of the International Double Reed Society* 3 (1975), pp. 31–32.

Ozi, Etienne. *Méthode nouvelle et raisonnée pour le basson*. Paris: Le Roy, 1787.

———. *Nouvelle Méthode de basson*. Paris, 1803.

Perdue, Robert E., Jr. "*Arundo donax*—Source of Musical Reeds and Industrial Cellulose." *Economic Botany* 12 (1958), pp. 368–404.

Popkin, Mark, and Loren Glickman. *Bassoon Reed Making*. Evanston, Ill.: The Instrumentalist Co., 1969.

Praetorius, Michael. *Syntagma Musicum*. Vol. II: *De Organographia*. Wolfenbüttel: Elias Holwein, 1619. Facsimile, Kassel: Bärenreiter, 1958–59.

Rothwell, Evelyn. *The Oboist's Companion*. Vol. III: *Reeds*. Oxford University Press, 1977.

Spencer, William G. *The Art of Bassoon Playing*. Revised by Frederick A. Mueller. Evanston, Ill.: Summy-Birchard Co., 1969.

Sprenkle, Robert, and David Ledet. *The Art of Oboe Playing*. Evanston, Ill.: Summy-Birchard Co., 1961.

Thompson, Stephen C. "The effect of the reed resonance on woodwind tone production." *Journal of the Acoustical Society of America* 66 (1979), pp. 1299–1307.

Virdung, Sebastian. *Musica getutscht.* 1511. Facsimile, New York: Broude, 1966.

Wangermée, Robert. *Flemish Music and Society in the Fifteenth and Sixteenth Centuries.* Translated by Robert Erich Wolf. New York: Prager, 1968.

Warner, Thomas. "Two Late Eighteenth Century Instructions for Making Double Reeds." *Galpin Society Journal* XV (1962), pp. 25–33.

Weait, Christopher. *Bassoon Reed Making: A Basic Technique.* Rev. ed. New York: McGinnis & Marx, 1980.

Weissenborn, Julius. *Fagott-Schule.* 1887. Translated and revised by Fred Bettoney. Boston: Cundy-Bettoney Co., Inc., 1950.

Westphal, Frederick. *Guide To Teaching Woodwinds.* Dubuque: Wm. C. Brown Co., 1962.

Weygers, Alexander. *The Making of Tools.* New York: Van Nostrand Reinhold Co., 1973.

White, Paul. "Early Bassoon Reeds: A Survey of Some Important Examples." *Journal of the American Musical Instrument Society* X (1984), pp. 69–96. Reprinted in *Journal of the International Double Reed Society* 16 (July 1988), pp. 71–92.

Winternitz, Emanuel. *Musical Instruments and Their Symbolism in Western Art.* New York: W. W. Norton, 1967.

INDEX

DAVID HOGAN SMITH edits and publishes music for wind instruments of the Renaissance and Baroque periods. He performs on early woodwinds and brasses and is the founding director of the King's Trumpetts and Shalmes, based in San Francisco.